MAGIC & MISTLETOE

Confessions of a Closet Medium, Book 2

NYX HALLIWELL

Magic & Mistletoe, Confessions of a Closet Medium, Book 2

© 2020 Nyx Halliwell

ISBN: 978-1-948686-34-1

Print 978-1-948686-35-8

Cover Art by EDH Graphics

Formatting by Beach Path Publishing, LLC

Editing by Beth Neal, Patricia Essex

Please Note

This is a work of fiction. Names, characters, places, and incidents are either the product of the author's imagination or used fictitiously, and any resemblance to actual persons, living or dead, business establishments, events or locales is entirely coincidental.

Your support of the author's rights is appreciated.

The magic of Christmas never ends
And its greatest of gifts
Are family and friends.

Chapter One

D ecember is my favorite month, Christmas my
favorite holiday.

It's only a few days away and Rosie and I are
decorating the front window of The Wedding Chapel with a
bride scene I woke up with front and center in my mind this
morning.

Aunt Willa would love it.

Hopefully, her spirit is hanging around and is delighted to
see my idea. Equally important is that if she is, she's also satisfied with how I'm running her event planning business.

Bing Crosby plays through the stereo speakers that my
friend, Brax, set up for the front area. Long ago, my aunt turned
her beautiful Victorian home into her office, opening the rooms
on either side of the grand door to create one big floor space.
Each side sports a giant bay window where displays of wedding
themes and other formal party events showcase the business's
offerings.

The three cats—Arthur, Lancelot, and Tabitha—laze by the
fireplace where the smell of wood smoke mixes with the fresh
scent of fir tree. Tabitha is grooming her marmalade colored

fur; Arthur and Lancelot watch her through sleepy-lidded eyes. Rosie has spiced cider brewing, the cinnamon and cloves recalling memories of holidays spent here with my beloved aunt.

The smaller artificial tree in her window is done in silver and blue, and we've spotlighted a snowy scene, filled with sparkling icicles and snowflake ornaments. The contemporary bride in that scene wears a dress from my line coming out in the new year, along with one of my aunt's faux fur wraps that resembles white mink. The prototype is a favorite of mine, and I'm still wrestling with the official name for it.

"The Madison?" I try it on for size. "It needs a modern name."

Rosie leans back and eyes it. She's wearing an ivory sweater with miniature jingle bells lining the collar. Every move produces a sleigh sound. She's tamed her thick, dark hair into a ponytail with a festive bow. "How about The Emery? It's on my list of modern baby names."

"Sort of sounds like a nail salon." My aunt used emery boards all the time. There's a stash in her antique desk I can't bring myself to toss yet. "Do I want to know why you have this list?"

She gives a sly smile. "Just dreaming a little."

Rosie and her husband have a five-year-old boy. The kid keeps her hopping and this is the first she's mentioned wanting to have another. "I can just see you running around with a miniature Rosie at your feet," I tease.

Her laughter is soft and wistful. "I've always wanted a girl. Maybe one of these days."

In the matching window, I'm stringing lights in a more vintage scene. With my boyfriend, Logan's, help, I've moved the grandfather clock into this large space and set the hands at midnight. The chimney and fireplace are made from cardboard but you wouldn't know it from the detail Brax and I painted on it.

Arthur meanders over and hops into the window, rubbing his lanky gray body across my leg. Rosie and I created a comfy scene with stockings hanging from the false, but very real-looking, mantle. Giant presents are wrapped in shiny foil, and all the touches are white with gold trim.

This bride-to-be sits in the midst of the gifts under the tree, the mannequin so lifelike, I almost feel as though I could talk to her. She's staring into a blue velvet box with a giant diamond ring inside, her handsome fiancé by her side. She's wearing a vintage lace dress I found in a closet upstairs. My mother claims it was once worn by my great-great grandmother.

Arthur hops in her lap, causing the fake ring box to jostle. "No, no," I say, gently removing him. Carefully, I check the dress for claw marks and am relieved to see none.

Rosie adjusts the wrap. "How about calling it The Bellamy?"

After wistfully making adjustments, wondering what it might be like to be proposed to at Christmas, I turn to eye the dress in Rosie's window. "Bellamy...hmm." I roll the name around in my head. "Ritzy, with kind of an old-world charm. I like it."

"Bel or Bella for short," Rosie says, trailing her fingers over the stole. "It's French and means beautiful friend."

"Pretty. I'll ask Brax and Rhys what they think."

The partners are our go-to for all things relating to fashion and business. She pins a poinsettia brooch on the white fake fur. "Good idea."

The outside porch and railing are festooned in evergreen garlands, twinkle lights, and shiny ribbons tied amongst the pinecones. Poinsettias decorate the steps to the wide porch and we've wrapped matching garlands around the outsides of each window. "Aunt Willa would love this."

From her spot in the window, Rosie nods. "She'd be very proud if she were here. You've done a great job with the place."

Making the decision to step into my aunt's shoes and take over her business was no easy decision. Moving home to Thornhollow? Even harder.

I can't believe she's gone, even after all these weeks since Halloween when I uncovered an ugly secret behind her death. Since then, however, I've relocated here from Atlanta, and for the first time in many years, I'm looking forward to Christmas. I haven't been this excited about the holidays since childhood.

Digging in a box for more lights, Lancelot sticks his nose in as if to help. Arthur has sidled up to the tree in the window and I shoo him away when I see him eyeing the ornaments. My imagination doesn't need help with envisioning him toppling the whole scene and causing me to lose my happy disposition.

"Logan alert," Rosie says, and her small chihuahua, Fern, begins barking.

Across the street a tall guy with wheat blond hair and a runner's build comes into view. Trailing behind him is Moxley, his Bassett hound, his long ears dragging on the sidewalk.

My heart gives a *thudthud* and my pulse keeps time with Bing's serenade.

Logan Cross is Thornhollow's only lawyer and he's a fine one at that. While this winter day in Georgia is barely below fifty, his wool jacket and plaid scarf suggest cooler temperatures.

There's only been three times in my life I remember having snow for Christmas, but once again my imagination takes over. How perfect would it be to stroll the downtown Christmas walk with snow on the ground and my gloved fingers entwined with his?

"What do you want me to do about the rent?" Rosie interrupts my daydreaming and throws a handful of tinsel on her tree. "We're late. Again."

Forcing my attention away from Logan, I shake out the string of lights in my hand. "What? I thought we paid him at the first of the month like usual."

At Rosie's admonishment, Fern quits barking, her tiny paws carrying her to a soft dog bed nearby. She roots around under the blanket and hides her head. "Penn still hasn't paid the second part of her bill, and the ball decorations wiped out what little cushion we had."

My stomach tightens slightly. Logan technically owns the house. Before she died, my aunt needed money to hire samples made of my wedding gown designs, unbeknownst to me. She used up her life savings and sold the house to him to come up with it.

I plan to buy it back, but until then, he's our landlord.

And apparently, we're broke.

Before he crosses the street, a neighbor stops him to chat and I take a relieved breath. Penny Calhoun-Reed is a small problem in the grand scheme of things, but still. We need to get paid. "Penn's husband still hasn't found a job?"

Rosie finishes off the tinsel. "No, and we won't see our money from the ball until after the ticket proceeds are tallied and we're cut a check."

The Mistletoe Ball is one of the biggest events in Thornhollow every Christmas. The Chamber of Commerce is in charge of it, and when I stepped into my aunt's life, I did the same into her shoes as president of the group.

All of this is still new to me, and I make a mental note that next year we should make them cough up at least a partial deposit for the decorations.

I've put Rosie in charge of the details, so I can attend with Logan and enjoy myself. She's done a great job, and the ball is going to be bigger and better than ever. We're raising funds to support a local small dog rescue, a charity near and dear to

Rosie's heart. She's put every ounce of her ingenuity into making it extra special.

"How much do we have?" I ask, fearing her answer. How am I ever going to reclaim the house if I can't even make rent?

"Three hundred and twelve dollars in savings, and close to a hundred or so in petty cash."

We're a hundred dollars short.

I chew my bottom lip, wishing sales from my wedding dress line were already coming in, but since Gloria and her company who sews them can't begin taking orders until January, I can't fully launch until then. My debut is scheduled for March; I'm excited and extremely nervous.

I need time. That extra income will all be put toward purchasing the house.

Across the street, Logan smiles at the man he's chatting with. He's so handsome, so perfect in all the ways that matter. Even the quirk of his mouth and his nod mesmerize me. The two share a laugh, and the man pats Moxley's head. A woman with a stroller goes by and waves.

Christmas cheer is in the air.

And so is a ghost of Christmas Past.

My stomach twists as I think about what I have to do before the ball. Not only do I need to talk to Penn, come up with rent, and give Rosie a bonus, I have to keep an awful secret from the man I love.

It's been nearly two months since his mother hired me to protect him from an unseen, yet deadly threat that will strike the night of the ball if I don't stop it.

The problem being, I have no idea how.

On top of that, I'm a horrible liar, and I've been dancing around this secret for too long.

Logan and the man shake hands, their conversation wrapping up.

I swivel one way, then the other, my daydreams about

Christmas crashing down around me. No wonder Logan's been acting sort of weird the past few weeks. I thought it was because he was keeping my Christmas gift a secret. In reality, he's probably wondering how to ask me about the rent.

I need to escape—and quickly before he and Moxley dash over here. I will not let another day go by without paying him.

Rosie adjusts her mannequin's hand. "You could do a couple of Saturday nights at the Thorny Toad. Your aunt always made extra cash at those."

Now my stomach cramps for an entirely different reason. 'Mena the Medium' was the Thorny Toad's resident ghost whisperer and regularly used her psychic abilities to help folks. I have her gift, although to me, it's more trouble than it's worth. "Over my dead body," I grumble.

But the thought lights up a few brain cells and gives me an idea. Upstairs in an old trunk is a black ledger my aunt kept with lists of clients and the money she charged them. She didn't give away her services for free, whether it involved clearing a house of unwanted spirits or advising expectant parents if they were having a boy or girl.

Helen Cross hired me to do a job with no promise of payment, no deposit. A job with dire consequences if I don't find a solution.

Might be time to remedy that.

Tossing the lights haphazardly onto the tree, I step from the window. "I have a side job I'm working on. Let me see if I can get an advance."

I bolt, Arthur and Lancelot diving out of the way as Tabitha strolls by, nearly tripping me. She disappears in the direction of the kitchen.

Grabbing my wool coat from a hook near the door, my hand brushes the fresh holly and pine boughs trimming the door, the idea continues to gel. Through the window, I see Logan push through the gate, the wreath hanging on it bobbing with the action. He waits patiently for the dog to join him.

Keeping the curse from Logan makes me extremely uncomfortable, but I swore to his mother to do so in order not to worry him. "I'll return as soon as I can. Tell him I'm running errands."

One of Rosie's hands goes to her hip. "Don't you think you should be honest with him? He'll understand about our lack of funds. It's only temporary."

My relationship with Logan is complicated, and I'm out of my comfort zone simply *thinking* about him as my boyfriend. I don't know if I should tell him about our financial troubles or not, quite honestly. Of course, he'd understand, wouldn't he? And yet, my father taught me that money has a funny way of changing things between people.

Since his family is one of the richest in town, the last thing I want is for Logan or anyone else to deem I can't handle my affairs on my own and am milking him for cash. I don't want things to change between us—our relationship is still too new and fragile.

Four days—that's all the time I have to figure out how to save him from his family's curse. Paying rent and throwing the Mistletoe Ball should be the least of my worries.

Aunt Willa, I could use some of your psychic abilities right now.

As if she's suddenly by my side, I hear her voice telepathically. *"Run!"*

Or maybe that's my own inner survival instinct. Entering the kitchen, I flinch when Tabitha screeches at me from the counter. She paws the carafe.

"I'm not your servant." Naughty cat, she's always begging for food and seems to have a penchant for coffee these days.

Tabitha founded the town back in the 1700s with my grandfather multiple times removed. She's as bossy as my own mama.

But if it weren't for her, I wouldn't have solved Aunt Willa's murder, and stopped the killer from doing more harm.

At the base of the cabinet, Arthur and Lancelot seat themselves and watch us, as if hoping they'll get something out of this deal as well.

I wave her off. "Get your own coffee, Grandma, and please don't run around naked if you shift and scare Rosie and Fern to death."

Not only is my ancestor on her seventh or eighth life as a cat, she can transform into human form when she wants.

Lancelot's gray eyebrows rise and I swear Arthur grins. Speaking of naughty cats…

It seems they might like seeing her naked, and I make a mental note to lock them out of the bathroom when I shower from now on. I narrow my eyes at them. "You two behave."

Just as I'm sneaking out, I hear the bell above the front entrance tinkle and Logan's deep voice greets Rosie. Quietly, I slip through the screen door and out to the backyard.

Who would've thought I'd ever be running away from the most handsome, successful guy in Thornhollow?

But it's time I have a chat with his mama.

One way or another, I need her help breaking the curse haunting—and hunting—her son.

Chapter Two

✧❦✧

Heading to the famous Cross vineyard, the drive through downtown is a happy sight, regardless of my situation at the moment. I love seeing all the Christmas decorations my neighbors have to spotlight their shops for the walk, and laugh at some outside of snowmen having a snowball fight and Santa Claus stuck in a chimney in the residential area.

The murky sunlight is struggling against low-hanging clouds, and I turn on a radio station playing twenty-four hours of carols. I pass various roadside signs advertising the Festival of Lights Walk, along with the usual advertisements about the winery.

The season should be a bonus for the Cross family's business, since I managed to negotiate with another local company that produces high-quality chocolates, and the two have created a partnership with gift baskets. I'm getting Mama one with a combo of the vineyard's award-winning merlot and the candy company's brandy-infused chocolate turtles.

As I leave the city limits, houses become spaced farther apart and I pass horse pastures and barns. Even here, the holiday season is in full swing. White picket fences are decorated with garlands and wreaths. Grander displays meet the eyes on open lawns. Farmhouses have lights in every window, the horses in the pastures also adding to the ambience.

According to Logan's mama, many details have been lost along the way, but the basic one remains. A witch came after her family two hundred years ago, and her great-great grandmother fought back. She managed to kill her and curse the woman's ghost into the locket I now possess.

Unfortunately, the spell is about to expire. When it does, that spirit is coming after Logan.

The very thought of it makes my hackles rise. I'll do whatever it takes to protect him and his family, I only wish I had more time. So far, I haven't found a single way to stop it.

"Persephone?" I call to my guardian angel. "I need help."

Crickets. I've been begging her to show herself and do what she's supposed to—guide me—since Halloween. What good is a spirit guide if she's not around when you need help?

I hum along as I take the drive up into the hills. I pass patches of ancient trees before the view opens up showing me rows of grapevines, now dormant. Fog lingers here and wends its way amongst the various acres. I'm not surprised to see the entire grounds and house done in expensive and classy holiday trimmings. No jolly Santas stuck here.

I park in the lot near the store where the wine tastings and special events are held. The old speakeasy barn resides in the distance, the fog hovering around the weathervane at the peak.

The first wedding I did after returning to town was an impressive affair, even for me to pull off. Because of an angry ghost who ruined the planned Country Club proceedings, Rosie and I ended up doing it here in the barn.

Talk about ghosts...even this far away I see and sense some near the building. The lingering memories and loops of time overlay the present like a vintage black and white film.

Gathering my courage, I make my way to the wraparound porch. A luscious fresh swag of spruce and red berries graces the old oak door. Sprigs of mistletoe are artfully arranged in it, and a matching potted tree is festooned with lights and velvet ribbons sits next to it.

Winston, the butler, answers my knock and escorts me into the large entry, offering to take my coat. "Ready for the holidays, Miss Ava?"

It makes me uncomfortable to have people wait on me, but the two times I've been here with Logan, it made Winston ill at ease when I *wouldn't* let him. I remove the necklace from the pocket before handing him the jacket. "I sure am. And you? Do you get to spend time with your family?"

A festive sprig of mistletoe with a red ribbon accessorizes his vest. "My vacation starts Friday. I'll be heading to Ohio that night."

"Happy holidays to you, then." I thank him profusely and he wishes me a Merry Christmas as he shows me into the parlor.

The room is chilly, no fire in the fireplace, but there is a fresh tree in the corner decorated with velvet ribbons and costly ornaments. It's beautiful and scents the air, but it lacks any personal touches and I wonder if Helen hired someone to decorate it.

Mama still to this day puts up the awful construction paper ones I made in elementary school. In amongst them, she hangs vintage baubles passed down from generation to generation. The Cross family has a long history, as evidenced by the rows of framed ancestor photos lining an entire downstairs wall, but there are no connections to the past on this tree.

Perhaps they keep a personal one in the less formal den.

Nearly ten minutes pass before Helen Caldwell Cross enters, her heels clip-clopping on the wood flooring. Dressed in pearls and a classic red dress, her platinum hair is curled and pinned high on her head.

She makes it obvious she wasn't expecting company, even though she's dressed in her Sunday best.

"I apologize for showing up unannounced," I say as she motions me to a chair. "I thought you might like an update on my research."

"Have you taken care of the problem?"

Helen is always direct, and it's usually a trait I admire. Today, however, it would be nice to see some emotion from the woman. "Unfortunately, no. I'm at a dead end."

Her lips thin. She paces to the rear window and peers out over her property. Pine boughs and mistletoe line the ledge. Rolling hills frame her profile.

Hands clasped, she pivots and gives me another harsh, impatient glare. "Try harder. We're running out of time."

Like I don't know? "I've studied tons of books, combed through articles on the internet for hours, talked to friends on the Pacific Coast who are experts on things like this, and well..." I lift my hands in *I don't know* gesture. "Even they're not sure what to do."

I hold up the necklace, the locket catching light from a nearby sconce. "I've even tried reaching out to the ghost and get no response."

Like a magnet, her gaze zeroes in on it, then darts away. "You have to do more. She'll suck out his soul if you don't!"

"Sounds awful, but how exactly can she do that?"

Helen braces a hand on the frame, jaw set. "This is your area of expertise, not mine. All I know is what I've been told."

I lower the necklace and jiggle it in my palm. "Tell me the story again about how your grandmother stopped the witch."

"We've been over it several times."

She doesn't like to discuss witches and magick, but I have to force the issue. "There has to be more to it, and anything you can remember might help."

Helen stalks from the window and drops into a deep

burgundy colored couch, crossing her legs and leaning on the arm. She stares into the fireplace, face rigid. "I've told you everything."

I don't argue; I simply wait. I've learned she resists being forced, and is stubborn as the day is long, as Aunt Willa used to say. If you give her a bit of time and space, though...

"The witch threatened our family," she begins, reciting facts she's already shared. "My great-great grandmother, Birdie May —a God-fearing woman—stood up to her. Things...happened."

"Fill me in on those 'things.'"

She huffs and fidgets, not taking her gaze off the cold fireplace. "The two of them were enemies from the start, and fought a lot."

"Over what exactly, do you know?"

"Land, I believe. Eventually, it led to the death of the witch on Christmas Eve, and my grandmother wasn't about to let her ghost haunt our family, so she cursed her into that to keep us safe. It's been two hundred blessed years of safety and protection from"—she points a well-manicured finger toward the locket—"that horrible, horrible person. Birdie made sure she couldn't harm her loved ones and burnt all of her stuff, even those disgusting dolls."

My intuition perks up. "What kind of dolls?"

A twitch of her fingers. "You know. The kind they stick pins in. The witch had lots of them that she used to curse people. She had one of Birdie."

I set the locket on the coffee table between us and eye it speculatively. "Like voodoo?"

Helen flicks invisible dust from her dress. "My grandmother burned them along with the other tools."

"Tools?"

Another huff, lips set defiantly. "A knife, I believe. Candles. You know, *witchy* stuff."

"Why didn't you mention this before?"

Her eyes, so much like Logan's baby blues, meet mine. Hers are cold and unforgiving. "I didn't think it consequential."

Maybe it isn't, but the doll angle gives me something more to check into. If Birdie's enemy was into black magick or voodoo, this is a fresh avenue to research in regards to the curse. "How did your grandmother kill her?"

Helen returns to staring. "No idea."

"How would she know the means to curse the ghost into an object?"

"She used the power of the Lord."

Of course, she did. If only that could help me now. "Is there anything else you haven't told me?"

A shake of her head causes frustration to rise once more. There's more to this story, I'm sure of it, and the facts could be key to breaking the curse and sending this spirit onto her next incarnation.

If that's even possible.

"Why Logan?"

I've asked her before, but she's always ignored the question. Today, I don't plan to let her off the hook. "I need to know for sure why he's the target."

Her erect posture deflates slightly at the mention of him. "The witch wanted a son and my great-great-grandparents had seven. She believed they took the land from her family so she wanted a male heir as payment. My grandmother wasn't about to give her any such thing."

"That was two centuries ago. How can you be sure when she's freed that she won't come after you or your mother, since you're both alive?"

Helen glances at me as if I'm daft. "She'll come after the youngest male descendant of the maternal Caldwell line."

Once again, I feel as though she's leaving out important details. I sit forward, placing elbows on knees, and give her an earnest look. These few crumbs of new information may not change anything, and I need her to understand the seriousness of failure. "Helen, are you sure there's a spirit trapped in there? If there is, and you're holding back other information, this could end badly."

Her gaze follows my finger as I point to the locket on the table.

Fear shows in her face when she turns back to me. "The curse is real, and I've told you everything. You have to stop this. You understand family curses, and I'll give you whatever you want, just..." Her eyes tear up and her voice quivers. "Please save my boy."

The Holloway family's curse could've killed my dad, but I managed to break it, and that gives me a unique status in her eyes. My success may also give her false hope that I can keep her son safe.

Luckily, my father is still alive and kicking, and can return to Thornhollow with no deadly consequences. I understand how terrifying this must be for her, and yet I don't understand why she'd withhold information.

The sound of my cell, still in the pocket of my coat in the hall, breaks the tension. It's Logan's ringtone, and I sigh, remembering the second reason I'm here. "I need money."

His mother blanches, and I figure she's assuming I'm milking her because of her wealth. Dignity aside, I have to ask for financial assistance because we're out of time and I can't be polite anymore, no matter how much Mama and Aunt Willa pounded southern manners into me. At least with Helen, I know she'll be discreet and no one will find out if I ask for a loan.

"I can't focus on this when I'm unable pay rent to your son."

Her lips twitch.

"Look, Rosie and I've had some financial struggles since I took over my aunt's business, but by January things will get better. There will be more cash flow, and I'll pay you back. Right now?" I shake my head. "I have bills and not enough funds. I can't even cover Rosie's salary, and it's Christmas. She deserves a bonus. She has a son, too, one she needs her paychecks for in order to buy gifts. I'm sure you understand."

In reality, I doubt Helen has ever struggled in either capacity. However, appealing to the mother in her is my best avenue.

Her hand grips the arm of the couch, her knuckles whitening. She pushes upright, and as I see the hard look in her eyes, I think she's going to throw me out.

Instead, she marches to an antique desk. From a drawer, she withdraws a blue bag and returns.

Unzipping it, she yanks out a stack of bills in a white paper sleeve. They're hundreds.

Breaking the sleeve, she meets my gaze. "How much do you need?"

Chapter Three

※❀※

Back in my car, I find Tabby waiting for me. One marmalade colored paw touches the necklace when I toss it on the passenger seat. "How did you get here?"

She blinks her gold eyes at me but doesn't answer. Occasionally, even in cat form, she speaks. She seems to enjoy her feline form more than her human one.

I saw her shapeshift once, and I have to say, I'm rather glad she doesn't do so often. Otherwise, she'd freak me out more than she already does.

She was a powerful witch in her time, though we don't talk about that in our family. I grew up believing, much like everyone else in town, that the founder of Thornhollow was simply an herbalist and midwife. Turns out, there was a lot more going on with her than most knew. Then or now.

She's not the only one I hear talking to me, and I believe some of that is due to the fact I had a near death encounter after I arrived home. Logan actually saved me and brought me back to life, so our relationship truly is complicated. I feel like I owe him on many levels—Tabitha too, unfortunately—and even breaking the curse that's haunted his family is not quite enough to reverse that.

Stashing the money in my purse, I start the car, ignoring the ghosts hovering nearby. Some are from the speakeasy era who are more aware than their counterparts simply going through the time loops. There are at least two that need help crossing over, but I don't have the availability or energy to worry about them today.

It's not like I simply open the door to heaven and push people through. Every ghost has a story, a reason they're anchored here, and I have so much on my plate at the moment, I can't take on even one more mystery to solve.

As Tabitha bats the locket onto the foot mat, I shoot her a look and pull around the circular drive. I'm thinking about how I'm going to pay Helen back. I'll need to advertise my wedding dress line extensively, and that takes funds. I've learned the old adage you need money to make money is true.

The weight of owing so many people so many things weighs heavy on my shoulders and I nearly miss the flash of Logan's red car shooting up the lane until it's nearly too late. He's coming to see his mother—or maybe chasing after me.

He didn't know I was coming here, so he must be checking on her. He's good like that, and it warms my heart when I think about how loving and devoted he is to his family.

He slows, and I see his driver's side window beginning to lower so he can speak to me. A big smile is on his face, and I swoon a little, knowing I'm totally in love with this guy.

But self-preservation kicks in and I panic. I can't expose why I'm here and I hate lying to him. To anyone.

My mind blanks. Still, I slow, waving jerkily, breath caught in my throat.

"Hey," he says, his smile making my stomach do somersaults. "You okay?"

"Yes, of course!" I'm nodding like a looney person. "Why?"

"You look pale."

"Didn't sleep great." This is true. "Haven't had enough caffeine."

He glances toward the house. "Visiting Mother?"

I swallow the pit in my throat. "Going over a few details for the ball."

Internally I cringe—his mother has nothing to do with the big event.

Wrinkles form at the corners of his eyes as he surveys my face. "I didn't realize she was helping you."

"Oh, you know, her taste in décor is extraordinary." This too is truth, but what I add is not. "I wanted her opinion on the table centerpieces."

From the long pause, I know he knows I'm lying. I stay as far from his mother as I can, regardless that he and I are dating.

"The gift baskets!" Helen and I actually discussed them two weeks ago, but Logan doesn't know that. "We discussed what to include in the ones for the fundraiser."

He nods, buying this one. "I'm sorry I've been so busy with all the end of year stuff. I should be helping you with the ball."

"I'm sorry about being late on rent. I have it, just...things have been..."

"Crazy," he finishes for me. "I know."

I reach my hand across the expanse between us. "We'll have plenty of time to catch up after Christmas."

He takes my hand and squeezes. "I'm holding you to it."

Out on the main road, I turn on my Bluetooth and instruct it to text Helen, relaying the lie that we were discussing the ball and gift baskets if Logan asks.

As I make my way toward town, I use it again to call my friend, Winter. She and her sisters are the witches I know in Oregon, and whom I rely on to help with all things magical.

They have an amazing shop filled with crystals, body products, tarot cards, and crafts. I'm so proud of all the work they've done, and how they're expanding their line and services.

I wish I could fly across the country to see them. With all this stress, being wrapped in sisterly hugs, and maybe having Summer do an energy session on me, sounds like my version of heaven. I'm completely out of balance, my nerves getting the best of me, and as Winter answers, the sound of her voice grounds me, keeping me from having an anxiety attack. "Happy Yule," she says.

"Happy Yule and Merry Christmas. Are you super busy?"

She chuckles with sarcasm. "Autumn's plans for the expansion are undergoing another addition, if you can believe it."

"I can." Thinking about all the amazing work they do for others lifts my spirits. "I can't wait to visit when it's complete."

"Did you break that curse yet?"

"You'd be the first to know if I did." Absentmindedly, I glance at a Christmas display in the Stockard's yard of two snowpeople locked in an embrace. The male holds a sprig of mistletoe above the female. "I'm still not sure what to do, but I did discover the witch used dolls. Any thoughts on that?"

"Voodoo?"

"That's my take on it."

"Hmm. Sounds like Mamma Nightengale's territory. Her mother and grandmother practiced it, although I'm not sure how much she knows. How about I have her call you?"

Tabitha meows, and I ignore her. "I'm desperate. Anything, or anybody, that has an idea, send them my way."

We disconnect and I stop at the Bee Hive diner to grab some lunch. I'm starving.

As I park in front of the large glass window advertising today's special, Queenie, the owner, is walking her last customer out. The two are talking a mile a minute and I smile as the woman leans over and hugs Queenie before they part.

"You take care, now, Bonnie," she calls and the woman waves

to her. "Happy holidays!"

On the sidewalk, I smile at her when she rounds on me. I make prayer hands in front of my chest. "Please give me something to eat for lunch. I've had a horrible morning and I'll owe you forever if you take pity on me."

"You already owe me your firstborn son." She looks down her dark nose at me, her lips in a scolding frown. "Who do you think you are showing up at closing time and expecting me to feed you?"

This wonderful woman has been like a second mother to me through the years. "Someone you love regardless of my short comings?"

Her frown disappears and she pulls me into a bear hug, then ushers me inside. Flipping the sign on the door, she takes the daily lunch special flyer out of the window and tosses it on the counter. "You're lucky I love you."

"Yes, ma'am. I am."

I take a bar stool at the counter, remembering when this was an ice cream shop. Brax's mother has redone it in a down-home atmosphere and talks a mile a minute as she waves her fry cook away and whips up a huge plate of food.

The fried ham and cheese, coleslaw, and side of hush puppies makes my mouth water and I can't eat fast enough. She slides a milkshake in front of me and I suck that up, too.

Queenie continues to clean and prep for the evening hours as she gives me the latest gossip. Since my mouth is full, I just nod and make noises.

"What about the ball?" she queries me. "Everything set for Saturday night?"

The backdoor squeaks as someone comes in and Brax's voice shouts, "I'm here, Mama."

The fry cook leaves, stating he'll be back in two hours to start the dinner special. I finish the sandwich as Brax greets his mother, then me, his giant arms nearly squishing me in a hug.

He helps himself to a large iced tea. "Can I get one of those?" He points to the tiny portion of sandwich I haven't finished.

"Ava was just about to fill me in on the ball," Queenie says, wiping her hands on a dishrag. "Sit down and I'll make it."

I use a napkin to wipe my mouth and place a hand on my extremely full belly. "Everything for the ball is set. I wish you were catering."

She waggles a finger at me. "My food ain't for the Country Club."

I sigh. "We have a few last-minute decorations, like the fresh mistletoe, and I'm waiting on a final count on the tickets sold, but otherwise we're good to go."

Brax dwarfs the stool, his big hands fiddling with his tea glass. "The most important question is, what are you planning to wear?"

Brax is always concerned about my appearance, maybe more so than my mother, if that's possible. He's been my best friend since we were toddlers and next-door neighbors. Our moms are also best friends.

Since he and Rhys bought the bed and breakfast last month, we're once again living beside each other. "I sketched a dress for the event, but I don't have the time or material to make it. I'll scrounge through my closet and find something presentable."

One dark brown eye winks at me. "Honey, if you've got a sketch, I'll take care of the rest. What's it look like?"

I pull out my phone and show him a photo of it. "Spaghetti straps, winter white chiffon, and a short raspberry colored velvet cape."

He whistles under his breath and Queenie eyeballs the sketch. "Looks like flapper-style meets sophisticated Christmas."

"The speakeasy wedding in October gave me lots of ideas for a whole line of Roaring Twenties wedding gowns. Thought I'd test drive one for the ball to see if it's workable."

"Workable?" Queenie smiles. "Honey, this is stunning. I can't wait to see it on you."

"Well, unfortunately, that's not going to happen."

"Sure, it will." Brax is confident and Queenie is smiling as she returns to the kitchen side. "And I'll do your hair."

I give him a questioning glance. "The ball is in three days. What do you have, a magic wand?"

His broad shoulders shake as he laughs, his deep voice echoing off the high ceiling. Queenie puts together a sandwich for him, smiling at the sound. "I know a gal who can sew it up quick. It'll be my Christmas present to you."

"Thank you, but that's not necessary. You and Rhys come over Christmas afternoon and share some of Rhys' good cooking with me and that will be enough. I've got plenty of old dresses that'll work."

Queenie brings his food and leans on the counter. She lowers her voice, eyes lit with expectation. "What about your mama and her secret beau? Do you know who it is?"

I frown. "What? Mama doesn't date."

One of Queenie's brows lifts. "You sure about that?"

"Not possible. She and Daddy are still married."

"They've been separated a long time, Ava." Queenie straightens. "She's lonely."

My father, a former cop, actually dreamed of being a rock star. Because of the family curse only my mother and aunt knew about, and the possibility he could die young because of it, Mama chased him out of town and told him to follow his dreams.

"It would be good for her to find someone who makes her happy," Brax says, but he's studying me closely, registering my reaction.

"Who told you she's bringing a date to the ball?" I question his mother.

She shrugs, fussing over a napkin holder nearby. "Heard it on the wind."

Which means Mama told her. Just not who this beau is.

"I can't believe it," I say. "How could she not tell me?"

One of Brax's hands lands on my arm. "The kids are often the last to know."

Queenie snorts and starts drying a glass. "She probably didn't want to upset you. And she seems to be keeping it from all of us."

"Who could it be?"

They both stare at me with blank faces. Out of the slim pickings of bachelors in town close to my mother's age, none seem a good fit.

A knock breaks the silence. Queenie's brows draw together in the center of her forehead as she skirts the counter, muttering under her breath, "Closed sign means closed. What is wrong with people?"

"Just ignore it," Brax advises.

"Oh dear." She's already at the door, and I hear her clear her throat. "Speak of the devil."

I can't see around her ample body when I swivel, but whoever it is, it can't be good by her tone. Probably one of the regulars who saw Brax and I, figuring they can take advantage of Queenie's soft heart.

Milkshake in hand, I take the last sip, thinking about interrogating Mama.

Queenie opens the door. "Well, now," she says, all fake friendliness. "Look what the cat dragged onto my doorstep."

For half a second, she's still blocking my view, then she steps back. The person is backlit on the stoop. It takes a moment for my eyes to focus, for my mind to register who I'm seeing.

"Hello, Queenie," the man nods at her, then glances my way.

He meets my eyes with a big smile. "Hello, Ava, girl."

Shocked, the last person I expected to see today stepping into the diner, I drop my glass.

"Daddy?"

Chapter Four

My father takes three long strides across the tiled floor, pulls me off my stool, ignoring the shattered glass at my feet, and hugs me like he hasn't seen me in an age.

He hasn't. In fact, with him on the road with his singing career so much in the past few years, we've barely connected in person. Video chats, calls, and texts are great, but there's nothing better than seeing him face to face.

I sink into his embrace, his familiar soap and aftershave engulfing me. Closing my eyes, I soak it all up.

"There's my girl," he says, rocking us slightly back and forth. "I've been waiting to do this for so long."

He was going to visit at Thanksgiving, but got a gig in Kentucky and didn't.

"Daddy." I breathe the word on a long sigh. We break the hug but not our contact, our arms around each other. "Why didn't you tell me you were coming?"

He squeezes my arms and takes my hands in his, moving us so Brax and Queenie can sweep up the glass. I apologize to her and she waves it off.

"Didn't want you to be disappointed if I couldn't make it," he tells me, "but I'm here now. I insisted to my manager I needed to be home for Christmas."

I'm thrilled, but in the back of my mind, I realize Mama's going to freak. She's been planning everything with a fervor I haven't seen in years, claiming this will be the most special holiday ever since I am home again.

But this is Dad. He's finally in Thornhollow again and I couldn't be happier. "You're staying with me. I have plenty of room at Aunt Willa's."

"Don't they feed you, Nash? You're too skinny," Queenie admonishes. "I'm making you some lunch."

"Don't go to any trouble for me," he insists, but he's smiling and winking.

"Good to see you," Brax adds.

As Queenie dishes up food in a to-go container, he and Dad share a man hug and promise to get together.

"I hear you bought the B&B," Dad says.

Brax tousles my hair, then smooths it back down. "Someone has to keep Ava in line."

We say our goodbyes and I accept hugs from Brax and Queenie. Dad follows me through town to The Wedding Chapel.

Rosie has finished the windows when we arrive. She and the cats greet us and I covertly give her the money for rent, while dad brings in his suitcases. She gives me the side-eye, but doesn't ask any questions.

Dad leans his guitar bag against his luggage and pulls out a neon orange pick. He hands it to her. "Like my new business cards?"

She reads the lettering as I glance at it over her shoulder. "That's really cool," Rosie says. "What a great idea."

"Nash 'The Phantom' Fantome," it reads with a gold star outline around the nickname and his website on the flip side.

I show him upstairs to a spare bedroom and pull out a set of fresh sheets. We chat about his last gig and the weather. He doesn't ask about Mama, and I leave that topic alone as well.

"Take your time settling in," I tell him. "I'll be downstairs if you need anything."

Rosie hands me a mug when I enter the kitchen. "Logan's suspicious about you sneaking out of here, and do I want to know how you're suddenly flush with cash?"

The cider is warm and tastes amazing. "I already spoke to him. Don't worry. It's Christmas—people are always sneaky this time of year, and he knows how busy we've been."

Ignoring the second question, I check the fridge for dinner possibilities. No magical entrees appear, and I realize it's been a while since I cooked anything. For weeks after Aunt Willa died, I was spoiled with the ladies' auxiliary constantly bringing food. I may have to break down and pull out one of my aunt's recipe books and try making something.

Tonight, however, pizza will do.

Rosie returns to her desk. Filling up on the cider, I sort of wish it was embellished with a little wine. I may need it with my parents, the curse, and my current financial situation bearing down on me.

Logan texts about a meeting he has and can we meet up beforehand for lunch. I tell him I've eaten and send a heart with it as an apology. As I pass Rosie, I compliment the finished windows. She smiles, always appreciating being recognized for her hard work. "Sure is great to have your dad here for the holidays."

I hear the underlying questions in her voice. "Sure is."

I sip more cider, sitting at Aunt Willa's desk and thumbing through papers. If only I didn't have the cursed necklace to deal with and Logan's life hanging over my head, it might actually be awesome to bring Mama and Daddy back together at Christmas.

But what about this secret boyfriend she has? Now I have to deal with that as well. "Have you heard anything about Mama having a new beau?" I ask.

Her eyes bug out under her bangs, her jingle bells making soft tinkling sounds when she shakes her head. "Miss Dixie has a boyfriend?"

I shush her, pointing to alert her to dad possibly hearing. She makes an *oops* face. Since she hears all the town gossip like Queenieif she doesn't know, it really *is* a secret. "I can't believe that," she stage-whispers across the room.

"You and me both, sister."

I can tell she wants more info but I have none to give her, so I shrug, hands in the air and she mimics the motion back.

We work for the next while in concentrated silence. Dad comes down, his guitar bag slung over his back and his cell in hand. He pockets it and stops in front of me. "Sweetie, Brax wants me to perform at some bar south of here called the Thorny Toad tonight. I'm doing some holiday numbers and a few oldies, nothing big. Have you heard of this place?"

Rosie and I exchange a look. "That's great," I say, wondering if the woo-woo patrons will welcome him. "The Toad is located in the old metal works building off the highway. I can take you if you want."

He waves off the offer. "I haven't been gone that long, Ava. I know where that place is. I'm meeting him in twenty minutes to see the setup. He says he has a guitar amp I can use."

He's always happiest when he has a new gig on his plate. "You'll be back for dinner?"

"I'll just eat there. I go on at seven."

Pizza for one then. "Okay, no problem. I'll come by and cheer you on later."

He kisses my cheek, heading for the front door. Tabby appears, trailing after him. She rubs his leg as he stops to pull on his jacket. Golden, moony eyes stare up at him.

"See ya later, alligator," he says.

The childhood goodbye makes me smile. "After while, crocodile."

It was always our thing, and I get up and hug him. As he leaves, I lunge for Tabby, stopping her from going with him. "What has gotten into you?"

She hisses, bolting from my grip and hitting the floor with a hard *whomp*. Heaving a sigh as she struts away, I watch Dad through the window as he hops in his silver Eldorado, the vehicle he's had for as long as I can remember.

Glancing at the desk, I mentally prioritize what I need to accomplish before dinner, starting with the research. Voodoo and cursed objects with ghosts... I tell myself there will be thousands of entries, and plenty with ideas on what to do when the curse expires.

As Dad pulls away from the curb with a wave, I return it, my mind going back to the curse.

I never realized such a thing could have an expiration date, but Helen has been insistent that two hundred years to the date from when her grandmother and the witch fought, it would disappear, releasing the spirit trapped inside.

In my mind, I keep seeing a genie lamp, and wonder if that's how the witch feels, waiting for someone to rub that locket and free her.

"Persephone, if you're playing hard to get, please stop. Whatever you want, whatever you need, please come help me with this problem. I'm desperate."

It's not my guardian angel who shows up however.

I'm still at the window when a red Porsche pulls into the spot Dad vacated. Logan gets out and pins me with a look through the window before he heads my way.

Chapter Five

"Hey," Logan says, kissing my cheek as I let him in. "Another busy day, huh?"

The scent of fresh air and his woodsy cologne engulf me. "Very. You too?"

The corner of his mouth tugs into a smirk and a teasing light enters his eyes. "Only when I was attempting to catch up with you."

I chuckle and nervously glance away. "Would you like some cider?"

He shakes his head. "I've got one last client today. Can we do dinner? Nothing fancy, just pizza or something?"

Relief flows through me. "You read my mind. I have so much going on right now, that you, pizza, and some time in front of the fire sounds perfect."

He pulls me in for a tight hug and a deep kiss. When he lets go, I'm still swimming in bliss and only after he leaves do I remember Dad.

Ah, well. I'll mention him to Logan tonight.

I spend the rest of the afternoon researching voodoo, curses, dolls used in witchcraft, and think about how to tell Mama that Dad's here for the holiday.

While Rosie handles phone calls and bustles around securing the final details for the ball, I catch myself daydreaming.

Since it's my first Christmas home in a long while, and I've never actually attended the ball, I want to be swept away by the enchantment of the evening, twirling in Logan's arms, and reveling in the fact we're a couple. I'm sure there must be a way to solve the problem of the ghost in the necklace.

I can't lose him, that's one thing I know for sure. Whatever it takes, I have to figure this out and protect him from whatever that ghost might be able to do to him.

Toying with the silver locket, I wonder not for the first time whether burying it, throwing it out back in the creek, or destroying the pendant itself might work. I have no evidence to suggest it would and Winter and I have discussed this at length.

You can't destroy a spirit, a soul. It has to go somewhere, so we either keep it contained, or get it to cross over to the after-life. I feel somewhat like Harry Potter, attempting to destroy a horcrux, and wish I had the sword of Gryffindor.

By six, the cats are going crazy for dinner. Rosie bugs out and the house is quiet except for a few creaks and moans I've become used to the last few months. I still hold out hope I'll see my aunt appear before me, but her ghost seems to be busy enjoying heaven or whatever form of hereafter exists.

This makes me both sad and happy. I miss her, but I'm glad she's at peace.

I feed the cats and order pizza — Logan's favorite sausage and mushroom on half, my chicken Alfredo on the other. I open a bottle of wine for me and check my supply of beer for him.

He arrives shortly before the food and we dig in while it's hot, relaxing in the living room. I have a small fire going, and it lights the area sufficiently to create a romantic ambience. Logan puts one arm around me as we eat and tells me about his day.

I'm relaxed and the meal is delicious, and I'm thinking about kissing him when the front door opens wide and Dad calls out, "Ava? You here?"

All thoughts of romance flee and I come to my feet, turning to look at him. "Dad? What happened? I thought you were playing at the Toad?"

He sniffs the air. "Smells like Vinnie's in here."

Logan glances over his shoulder, "Dad?"

"Logan, you remember my father."

The two shake and Dad smiles at him. "Logan Cross. Good to see you, young man."

As he shrugs off his coat and lays it on the arm of a chair, Logan flicks a glance at me. "Mr. Fantome, I didn't realize you were in town."

"Call me Nash. Ava mentioned you've been hanging around." He glances at me. "We had to cancel. The amp blew a fuse. Any left?"

I wave him toward the kitchen. "Help yourself."

He disappears in that direction and I quietly explain to Logan about his unexpected appearance and that he's staying with me through Christmas. I see a touch of disappointment on Logan's face and realize he had some romantic intentions for tonight as well.

Dad returns, sans plate, slice in his hand. As we resume our seats, he tosses a guitar pick business card at Logan and flops down across from us. He kicks his feet onto the coffee table, displacing a bridal magazine. "My daughter is a special gal," he says, directing this at Logan.

Logan pats my leg. "That she is."

Tabitha appears and licks her lips, jumping up next to my dad and staring at him. He wipes his fingers on his jeans before petting her. "I'm only going to say this once. You so much as cause my baby girl to frown, Cross, and I'll make mincemeat out of you. We clear?"

All the time he says this, he's smiling and eating. My dad, the epitome of good cop/bad cop all in one.

Logan's hand freezes, then withdraws. "Yes, sir."

"Daddy," I chastise. "Don't be rude. And by the way, I can handle myself."

He winks at me. "I know you can, baby, but it's good to keep the boy in his place."

I can't help but grin. "I'm sorry you couldn't play tonight. I know you were looking forward to it."

One eye narrows at me, letting me know I'm not as smooth as I think about changing the subject, but he's a sport and plays along. I'm sure I'll hear more about Logan and how I need to keep him on his toes later. "No biggie. Looks as though a few of my old bandmates are back as well. Maybe we'll get together, reminisce, do a few songs around town before the New Year. Might be fun."

I comb my memory for names and faces of the Fantome Phantoms—Dad's original band. Sean O'Reilly, the former drummer works at the Toad as a bartender. Last I heard, the base player, Sadie Calhoun, moved to South Carolina. Travis Wooten, the keyboardist died in a motorcycle accident. Were there more?

Dad stares at the fire, nostalgia in his eyes as it throws shadows across him. "Even saw a couple groupies there from back in the day."

I frown. "You had those here in Thornhollow?"

He winks.

Ugh. "You mean women who trailed after you and tried to get backstage passes?" I can't keep the innuendo out of my voice as images of barely clad young women flirting with my dad flash across my mind. "Pretty sure I didn't need to know that."

"I only ever had eyes for your mother, you know that. There are a few who followed us around. One or two even tagged along when we hit the road."

My father's always been a good-looking guy with a lopsided grin and a gravelly voice. I shouldn't be surprised he had female admirers, but I have to admit I'm relieved to hear he never cared about them.

He's still in love with Mama. The thought warms my heart. I'm no matchmaker—heck, I can't even handle my own love life —but sparks of ideas about how to get them back together race through my head.

Dad tenses, his head swiveling to look toward the front door. He jumps to his feet, making Tabby cry and hop down. "Your mother's here," he announces, smoothing his shirt and wiping at the corners of his mouth,

I stand as well, panic starting in my belly like butterflies. "What? Where?"

The doorbell rings.

Logan and I follow Dad's gaze to the entrance. I can see the faint outline of people on the dark porch.

Dad starts toward it and I brush past him. "It's not Mama," I tell him, hoping I'm right. "She doesn't ring the bell. She just walks in."

Mentally reassuring myself, I throw open the door. My stomach falls. I try to block her view of the interior. "Mama? What are you doing here?"

A sly smile crosses her face. A couple inches shorter than me, she's dressed in her usual two-piece suit and low heels. She's thrown a wool jacket over her shoulders and pinned a laughing Santa face to the scarf at her neck. "Hi sweetie. We're going to see the downtown lights and thought we'd stop by and invite you and Logan to come with."

We? Next to her is a man dressed in worn jeans, black motorcycle boots, and a leather jacket. His nose is red and his skin sags with wrinkles, suggesting a lot of alcohol and stress has been poured into his system through the years.

Sean O'Reilly. Floating slightly behind him in the dark is a ghost. When I stare at it, it grows darker, features rising on the face. There's something about it that seems familiar.

"Dixie?" Dad's voice has a curious note as he steps behind me.

Mama's face falls. She stares over my shoulder. "*Naaash?*" Her heavily accented voice draws out his name in shock.

"Hey, man," Sean says to my dad.

I keep my focus on the ghost, but it begins to fade.

Mama grips the scarf tightly. "What in the world are you doing here?"

My brain puts two and two together and my stomach twists. Her new beau is...

If I'm not careful, this will go bad fast. I force cheer into my tone. "Daddy's here for Christmas, Mama. Surprise!"

Chapter Six

Everyone starts talking at once.

Mama to Daddy: "Answer me. What are you doing here?"

Dad to Sean: "Are you seeing my wife?"

Sean to Mama: "Maybe I better wait in the car."

Mama to Sean: "You'll do no such thing."

Then to me: "How could you not tell me he was here?"

Finally, she rounds on Dad. "*Ex*-wife."

Dad begins to argue, Sean tries to hide a smile.

"Wait." My voice rises. "You're divorced?"

Silence ensues after the combination of incredulous shock and the loud announcement.

Logan comes up behind me and kisses the back of my head. "I'll call you later."

Coward.

Honestly though, I can't blame him. Family politics are a nightmare no matter who's involved.

Jacket in hand, he scoots around the rest and leaves, nodding to Mama and Daddy as he does. As soon as he's out of earshot, the others escalate once more into bickering, each trying to outdo the other.

"Calm down," I insist. "Let's talk this out reasonably."

No one listens. Mama points her finger at Dad's nose. "You have every right to see your daughter whenever you choose, but you have no say in my life."

"I do when you're dating him!" Dad points at Sean.

Sean disputes it and more squabbling ensues until I whistle loudly, cutting them off.

Three sets of eyes land on me. "Enough!" I make sure they know I'm serious. "It's Christmas, for heaven's sake. This is my house, and you will all respect me and one another by speaking calmly and politely. You two"—I point at my parents—"to the kitchen. Now." To Sean, I smile with all the southern grace I can muster, which isn't much at the moment. "Would you mind waiting outside?"

Good thing he doesn't disagree. I don't want him in here with his ghostly friend, whoever or whatever it is. He doesn't look particularly upset, and simply offers a shrug. But he winks at Mama, which causes that slight smile to rise to her face again, and makes my dad tense, before he saunters off the porch.

"Ava..." Mama starts.

I raise a finger, drag her inside, and close the door. "Kitchen. Now."

With some grumbling and side glances, they relent. Once we're in the brighter room, I pour Mama a glass of wine and open a beer for Dad. "Sit," I command.

Both open their mouths to argue and I raise the same finger to shush them.

Mama unbuttons her coat but resists when Dad attempts to help her remove it. They down several gulps of their respective beverages, Mama shooting glares at me.

I'm gonna need a drink, too. I grab my glass from the living room and refill it, then seat myself across from them. Taking a deep breath, I once more muster some of the grace and patience I've learned to use with them over the years. "Let's start with when you got divorced and why neither of you told me."

Mama takes a long sip then huffs. "It was ages ago. I didn't mention it because you were in Atlanta and were always so busy."

"It's barely been a year," Dad corrects.

He looks rather forlorn now, his gaze focused on Mama like Tabby's were on him earlier.

She makes a dramatic flourish with her hand and rolls her eyes. "You've been gone a long time, Nash. We both needed to move on."

The pizza in my stomach burns like acid. I direct my attention to her. "My living in Atlanta is no excuse, Mama, but that's water under the bridge right now. We're all here and I want us to get along. No arguing, no bickering, and you will be civil to each other, no matter what, you understand?"

She turns on Dad. "I was lonely. Wilhelmina's death made me realize I need fun and companionship in my life. I will not apologize for socializing with Sean."

Her chin raises in defiance. Dad appears slightly disgusted, but the sadness in his face doesn't leave.

My heart feels wounded. The reason Mama sent him away was because of that rotten family curse. When I managed to break it, I was harboring hope like any child of a broken marriage— that my parents might get back together. Being an adult doesn't change that.

Dad must have clung to that dream as well. He stares Mama straight in the eye and gives her a weak smile. "You deserve happiness, Dixie, that's for sure."

Then as he stands, he drops a loaded bomb. "But the honest truth is, I've never stopped loving you...and I never will."

Chapter Seven

✦❋✦

That night in my room I call Logan.

"How'd it go?" He asks.

I haven't seen Dad since he left us at the table. Mama stood in a huff and did the same without saying another word to me.

"My parents aren't speaking to each other, and I'm not sure if either is speaking to me at this point. They're so stubborn, especially Mama. I know in my heart she's never stopped loving him, and now she has a chance to be with him again. She's acting like a teenager over Sean, and…"

I trail off when my phone alerts me to an incoming call from Winter. In all the drama, I haven't had a chance to get back to the pressing matter of the curse. Time to put family business aside and deal with that instead. "Hey, I'm sorry, but I've got to go. Will I see you tomorrow?"

"You bet. Sleep well. And don't worry about your folks. Things will work out."

Wish I had his optimism. I disconnect with him and answer Winter. She and another woman smile at me from the video chat screen.

"Hey, girl, I know it's late on the East Coast." Winter's hair is pinned on top of her head, a cascade of curls resembling a dark waterfall. Around the base is a sparkling bandanna. The lady next to her has creamy brown skin, wrinkles, and green glitter eyeshadow.

"Hey, Winter. Hello, Mamma Nightengale." I smile, welcoming the reprieve from the drama of my family. "Good to see you both. It's not too late, I'm still up."

Mamma leans a little closer. "I hear you got some trouble brewing," she says. "Something about an old witch?"

I assume Winter has given her an overview of my situation but I touch on the important facts to make sure we're all on the same page.

"Where's Persephone?" Winter asks.

Persephone originally was Winter's guardian angel. The two didn't get along, and I ended up with her. She's extremely quirky—and now, unreliable. I've been calling for her since this whole thing started. "Good question. She's still AWOL."

Winter shakes her head, her curls swinging. "I'm so sorry."

"The worst part," I say, "is that the spell is about to expire. I'm running out of time to figure out how to stop it from coming after Logan."

Mamma Nightengale scratches at her cheek. "You're sure there's a ghost in that necklace?"

The item is across the room on my dresser. I glance at it. "I haven't felt anything supernatural from it, so honestly, I can't swear to that, but why make up such a story?"

Neither woman has an answer. Mama shrugs. "Well, voodoo or not, the way I see it, you have three options."

"I'm desperate." I roll my hand at her screen presence. "Hit me with them."

She nods and holds up a finger. "At the moment the hex expires, you can do another to seal the witch's ghost for another two hundred years. Two,"—she raises a second with a flourish, this one with a vintage ruby ring—"find some leverage to black-mail her into leaving your man alone. Three, you force her to cross over before she knows what happened to her."

I stare at her raised digits, excitement about having options dwindling as I realize how difficult all those things are. I knew this wouldn't be easy, but where is that magic wand when you need it? "Doesn't a spirit have to choose to move on? How would I force her to do it?"

"That's where you'll need help," Winter offers.

"I'm pretty sure I need help, regardless of which option I choose."

She gives me a sympathetic smile. "Options two and three work well together. If we can figure out a way to give her spirit something other than Logan, we can encourage her to coop-erate and travel onto the afterlife."

"Like what?" I rack my head for ideas. "She wanted a son—I can't exactly manufacture one in place of Logan."

Silence falls. "We're definitely not trading souls," Winter says. "That's dark, dark magick."

Definitely not going there. "What do you think she'll do to him?" Mama asks.

"That's another murky question. Mrs. Cross thinks she'll kill him and suck out his soul. Her words, not mine."

Winter makes a face that mimics exactly how I feel—as if I want to vomit.

"Maybe after all this time, she'll be happy to cross over." The bangles on Mama's arms clink as she turns her hands palm up. "After being trapped all those years, I sure would."

This gives me a boost of optimism. "Maybe you're right. I could be worried for nothing."

Winter pulls that rug out from under my sock-clad feet. "If I'd been hexed for any amount of time into an object, I'd be out for revenge. From the sounds of it, your witch isn't the type to turn the other cheek. You have to be prepared."

"The ghost of a vengeful and powerful witch is about to wreak havoc on my boyfriend." My voice has an edge of hysteria. "Did I miss the memo on how to stop that?"

The two exchange a look.

"You have to brace for all possible outcomes," Winter tells me gently.

"We'll help you anyway we can," Mama adds.

I drop my face into my hands. "Please tell me you have the magic wand that handles this."

"No," Winter says, "but we do have spells."

"I don't know how to do one."

"Yes, you do, girl. It's in your blood. Now grab a pen and paper. Here's what you'll need."

Chapter Eight

Armed with a renewed sense of hope and a list of items Winter told me to gather for protection, I make dad breakfast the next morning to cheer him up.

His favorite chocolate chip pancakes are a specialty of mine, and I dab extra whipped topping on his. I serve him coffee the moment he comes into the kitchen.

He's delighted and kisses my cheek. "Haven't had these in ages."

His joy in digging in makes me happy. As they're a favorite of mine, too, dad and I indulge while Arthur and Lancelot circle our feet, crying and begging for their own.

"It's so nice to have you home," I say around a mouthful. Washing it down with coffee, I revel in this moment, just me and him.

The cats meow and Dad bobs his head, swallowing. "Nice to be home. We have a lot to catch up on."

We text and call regularly, so I wonder what he hasn't told me. "Like what? You and Mama's divorce, perhaps?"

He waves his fork through the air. "Not about me. You."

Slippery slope there. "I'm great. Never thought I'd be happy living back here, but I am."

His elbow rests on the table and the fork points at me. "What about Logan? The two of you seem more serious than you let on."

Arthur paws my leg and I gently shoo him off. "Don't be silly. We're just...good friends."

"You're more than that."

True, but I don't know how to say it. I feel like a teenager with her first boyfriend. "Friends who kiss once in a while."

Dad chuckles. "He's a good kid. His family may be challenging, though."

"Tell me about it." I suck in a breath at the words and try to take it back. "I mean, they're nice and all. I like them."

I nod to try and give my weak declaration more oomph.

"Nice?" Dad gives me his knowing smile. "That word is the kiss of death when your mother uses it to describe someone. It means she can't stand them and is only being polite. From what I remember, Helen Cross is not *nice*."

Lancelot rubs my calf, meowing loudly. I chuck my napkin and rise. "All right, all right. Enough."

Avoiding Dad's mischievous eyes, I go to the stove and begin making a pancake without the chocolate. Tabby strolls in and sits staring at Dad. She purrs so lustily, I can hear it three feet away. "Let's get back to you and Mama," I suggest. "How do you plan to win her back?"

My directness takes him by surprise and he lowers the fork, moving pieces of food around on his plate. "Haven't figured that out yet."

"Is that the real reason you're here?"

His steady gaze meets mine. "I came back to see you first and foremost. I feel terrible about missing Thanksgiving with you."

I flip the pancake and rest a hip against the counter. "Water under the bridge. You're here now and that's what's important."

He sips his coffee. "Any thoughts?"

"On how to win over Mama?" I screw up my mouth, thinking. "She's a romantic at heart, so flowers, chocolates, compliments. You know, the usual. Don't mention anything about your competition, and be casual about it. Drop by City Hall and see if she needs help with work stuff. Invite her to lunch. Find the perfect time to say you're sorry and she was right."

"Sorry for what?"

"Doesn't matter. Relationships are full of little slights and hearing an apology and the words, 'you were right' will cause her to lower her walls and see you differently."

A shake of his head. "I don't get it."

I break up the cake and wave a hand over the pieces to speed up the cooling process. "Look, I'm no expert on relationships, we both know that, but I am on Mama. I've taken care of her a lot since she sent you away. Even though she's independent and wants everybody to see her as a leader, she secretly craves being loved." I toss the pieces in the three cat bowls and the felines descend on them. "We all do. Let her know she's appreciated and she'll be putty in your hands."

I return to the table to finish my breakfast and Dad looks pensive. I inquire about his last gig and that lightens the air. He keeps up a steady stream of stories and tells me about the lyrics he's working on. He seems truly excited about all of it, and doesn't mention Mama further. I don't either.

As I'm starting to clear the dishes, someone knocks. Out on the porch, I find Rhys in green trousers and a red vest.

"Morning, honey! I made cinnamon apple cake for our lone guest at the B&B this morning and had some left." He hands the wrapped loaf to me and kisses my cheek. It's still warm and I inhale the lovely aroma. "Thought you and your daddy might like it."

Rhys and Brax seem to enjoy running the bed and breakfast next door, as well as managing the Thorny Toad. Rhys is as good at creating alcoholic drinks as he is baking. This morning, his fair skin is flushed, accenting his freckles. He's obviously left a warm, toasty kitchen.

The air is chilly and I motion for him to come in. "Do you have time for coffee?"

"Not really, but I'd like to say hi to your daddy."

I lean close and lower my voice. "You didn't tell me Sean was seeing my mother."

Rhys draws back and frowns. "Our Sean?"

"The very one."

He covers his mouth in mock horror. "With your mother?"

I nod. "You didn't know?"

"Honey, I had no idea. That boy must get around."

"Why? What do you mean?"

"Sean has a girlfriend, I know that, but it ain't your mama."

"Seriously? He's two-timing her?"

Rhys nods. "There's been a gal real regular like when he works at the Toad. Haylee Dean Bower. She's related to Reverend Stout. His niece or something."

I want to punch Sean in the face. "To make matters worse, Sean is Dad's former drummer."

Rhys' expression shows a new level of shock. "No! I didn't know that."

"Dad's pretty hurt about it."

Rhys glances toward the kitchen. "What are you going to do about it?"

I fiddle with the wrapping on the cake. "I have no clue."

"Sean keeps things close to the vest, but he's been hitting the bottle hard. Comes in hung over a lot."

"Great."

As we enter the kitchen, Rhys and Dad exchange hellos.

Rhys stops near the fridge. "The electrical is all fixed," he tells Dad. "We'd love to have you play tonight." Rhys shoots me a glance, as if he's wondering if that's smart now that he knows about Sean. "That is, if you're interested."

Dad wipes his fingers on a napkin and tosses it in the garbage can. "Sure, I'll be there. What time?"

They settle on the details as I start washing dishes.

Rosie arrives, Fern in tow. There's one pancake left and she helps herself to it and coffee, greeting all of us. She breaks off a tiny bit for Fern.

Rhys leaves, Dad bugs out to go upstairs, and I hear him practicing a minute later. Rosie and I go to work.

My mind is filled with all the responsibilities hanging over me, and I can hardly focus. An hour later, the smell of cinnamon still hangs in the air. Dad jogs down the stairs and tells me he's going out for lunch. "The old band members are getting together at Queenie's."

I wonder if this includes Sean? "Have fun," I say and watch him leave.

After Rosie and I finish our morning appointment, I take off to a town eight miles away—the closest I could find to gather the items on the list Winter gave me.

The various ingredients are for a protection spell, a binding spell, and a ritual to put the genie back in the bottle if she won't cross over.

My aunt had a few of the herbs, but not the black salt or chalk to create the circle to hold the spirit while I decide what to do with her when the time comes. Maybe by then, I'll have a better idea, but for now, I have to be prepared to contain her so she can't hurt anyone.

I'm carrying the necklace in my pocket when I enter the store called Chicks with Gifts Emporium. Up to this point, the locket has never done anything, and I stewed all night about Mamma Nightengale's comment. Helen is certain it contains the ghost, but what if she's wrong? What if the family tale is just that—fiction?

As I enter, the smell of patchouli and lavender coil in my nose. My shoulders relax and I let go of an audible exhale.

"Welcome." The woman behind the counter has orange tipped pixie hair and is wearing a peace sign t-shirt. "I'm Raven. Can I help you?"

She comes out from behind the counter, heading toward a display with boxes of tarot decks in hand. On the table are fake crows and skulls, with an assortment of Christmas lights wound between them.

My coat pocket begins vibrating. Surprised, I slap a hand over the outside. "I hope so," I answer, digging in my bag for the list. "I need supplies for a..."

Her eyes brighten. "Spell?"

"Yes," I admit. "A couple actually. All very important."

"Oh, goodie," she says.

Before either of us moves, the necklace skyrockets out of my pocket and flies through the air.

Chapter Nine

"How intriguing," Raven says as it whizzes past her and catches awkwardly on the upright hand of a porcelain witch figurine. "What is it?"

With a sigh worthy of my mother, I edge toward the statue. "A pain in my backside."

Reaching for the locket, I flinch when it jets straight up, knocking into a decorative hanging lamp, then buzzes past a collection of goddess statues. It bumps one hard enough to cause it to tumble, and it tips into a display of feathers and smudging bowls, before landing on a holiday arrangement of jewelry. The entire exhibit of necklaces tumbles to the floor.

The locket seems to take a breather among its fallen comrades and I wonder if it's trying to use them as camouflage.

If I had doubts about the thing being possessed, I don't now.

"Sorry," I say, scrambling to fix the mess. "It's never done anything like this before."

"Haunted object?"

She seems knowledgeable about these things. "A cursed ghost is trapped inside."

"Hmm." The corners of her lips slant down. "That's different. How did it happen?"

Seems I'm repeating the story more than I care to lately. While I share what I know, I nonchalantly move toward the locket. It seems to quiver, and I freeze thinking it's going to bolt again.

"Clever," Raven murmurs once I finish. "I should use that on my enemies."

At my look of astonishment, she chuckles. "Kidding. The witch who cursed the ghost into the necklace must have been quite powerful."

"According to my source, she wasn't a witch, but a God-fearing Methodist."

"Sure." Raven snorts. "Sorry, not buying that one."

She asks me to wait and disappears behind a beaded curtain. I think about Helen's grandmother and wonder if she really was a religious woman, or if hers included a bit of magick.

I certainly wasn't prepared to find out my distant grandmother was a witch, and a shapeshifting cat on top of it. I imagine during that particular time in history, they kept their practice and the evidence under wraps. What better way than with religion?

I keep my eyes on the necklace, staying where I am, and scan the inside of the emporium since I have a moment to study it. The high-ceiling rafters exhibit bunches of drying herbs, antique birdcages, and vintage chandeliers. A collection of artistically embellished straw brooms covers one wall.

From the corner of my eye, I catch several ghosts moving around. I decide to ignore them, like I did the one attached to Sean and those at the Cross vineyard. I have enough to deal with without worrying about random spirits who might try to get my attention.

Raven returns carrying a black box with sigils burned into

the wood on all sides. Along with that, a pair of long handled tweezers.

She utters words under her breath in what sounds like another language, and the hair on the back of my neck rises.

At the same time, the necklace seizes up, going rigid.

Using the tweezers, she lifts it and places it in the box. "There." Shutting the lid, she smiles and hands it to me. "That should keep it under control for now."

"How did you do that?"

"It's called a curse box. It should be able to contain the necklace without any issues."

That was one of the items on my list. "That's amazing. Thank you. So even if the spirit gets free of the locket, this box will hold it?"

"Not exactly. To deal with the ghost, you're gonna need Tansy, Blessed Thistle..."—she goes to an apothecary-like shelving unit filled with bags and glass containers. Her black-painted nails and silver rings flash under the lights as she sorts through them. "Ah, here we go." She pulls several out and places them on the counter. "Black salt and witch's grass."

She adds more items to the collection and I'm thankful I've brought extra cash.

"Do you know how to perform an un-hexing spell?"

I move forward and set the box next to the herbs. "Un-hexing?"

"You can't send the curse back to the originator, since I assume she's dead."

I confirm with a nod.

"You have to undo it, then, and banish the spirit, but it would be best if you allowed a trained witch to handle that. This stuff isn't for the uninitiated."

The banishing the spirit part is where I keep getting hung up. "I assume you've done this before."

She lifts a shoulder and lets it fall. "Once or twice."

"When you say banish, you mean force a spirit to cross over, right?"

She leans on the counter. "This isn't a simple pesky ghost you can coax into moving on."

Her serious green eyes appraise me and she tilts her head. A moment passes where I feel a current of electricity snap between us, as though she's sending feelers into my aura.

Her head straightens and a knowingness comes into her eyes. "You're a spirit walker, aren't you? New to it, though."

My recent near-death experience puts me in that category, despite the fact I've seen ghosts since I was little. "Yes, long story. I see and communicate with the dead. I don't want to send this one out into the world, because she is malicious by all accounts and putting her down there..."—I point at the floor —"isn't something I'm comfortable doing."

She mimics my gesture. "*Down there* may not be exactly what you've been taught it is. You definitely need an experienced witch to help you with this."

"I'm almost out of time and my witch friend is on the West Coast."

She rings up my purchases and I mentally cringe at the total. "If you break the hex, you'll have a minor amount of control over the spirit itself. Then you can decide what to do with it, but you don't have many options."

"Can I hire you?"

She accepts my payment, then removes a crystal necklace from a display in the glass case and drapes it over my head. "This is a protection amulet. On the house. My sister, Sage, is the hex-breaker in the family. If you leave your name and number, I'll have her call you."

I scribble the info on a piece of a paper she provides, feeling the crystal on my collarbone beginning to warm.

Raven slides the info under a gargoyle statue next to the register. She tosses the pen into a cup shaped like a cauldron. "If you know any of the names of the original people involved, go next door and ask for Paris, the librarian. She'll know I sent you."

She walks me to the door. "Tell her you need information on dark magick witches in this area from two hundred years ago. See what she can unearth in her catacombs, okay?"

Feeling slightly more confident, I thank her and leave. At the car, I place the box and bag inside and eye the building next to the shop.

Small and quaint, the library is decorated with a smattering of holiday lights and bows. In the window, several colored flyers showcase story time with Santa and a Yule log-making party.

Raven comes out and points toward the car's windshield. "Is that your familiar?"

Glancing over my shoulder, I'm shocked to see Tabby on the dash, scrutinizing us. "Do you have a curse box that can contain her?" I grumble.

She chuckles. "Another pain in your backside?"

If she only knew. In normal company I would keep the details to myself. With her, I suspect she'll understand. "She's one of my ancestors who prefers life as a spoiled cat."

"Who wouldn't?" Another chuckle. "My two cents? You should invite her to work the spells with you."

I swear Tabitha winks at her, and Raven gives a wave and retreats inside.

The interior smells of leather and old paper, roses and knowledge. Magick tickles my nose. Two kittens wrestle in a large round bed, batting a ball of string between them.

Bestsellers in multiple genres line the shelves on both sides as I step deeper into the building. Across the carpeted space, I pick up hushed conversations and spot a wheeled cart lined with returns. Several books float off and land upon a nearby shelf, sliding themselves into place.

A ghost? Either that, or the librarian has some pretty cool

magick. I don't see or sense a spirit presence, and I pass by the magickal re-shelving unit on my way to the main area.

A circular desk comes into view as I pass the cart and a young woman with long, chocolate brown hair and rosy cheeks looks up. "Hello, Avalon," she says with a smile. "I've been waiting for you."

Behind her, the clear apparition of an older woman with cats-eye reading glasses and a matching smile waves to me. "Hello, Avalon."

Chapter Ten

Paris Charnel and her ghostly counterpart lead me down steep narrow stairs into an underground library, nearly identical to the one above, but filled with books on magick. The three of us pass endless rows, the periphery of stacks disappearing into shadows.

"Here it is," Paris stops and reaches toward a shelf, and a dusty tome wiggles out of the stack. "Witch Wars of the South, Fable County, Georgia, 1800s."

The volume is as long and wide as Rosie's tote bag.

I would love to spend the rest of the day down here, educating myself. Who knew there was so much going on in the unseen world that it has its own library? I'm astounded.

The air is denser, the shadows lit by sconces on the wall that come to life as Paris passes them. There's a heavy layer of ghosts, including two kittens wrestling with a ball of string. It's almost as if the library has a mirror self here.

One of the ghosts acts indignant at us for disturbing the quiet. He sits at a small table, stacks surrounding him. A goatee trims his face and small, wire rim glasses accentuate his somber eyes. His attire makes me think of the early 1900s.

Using an index system I can't begin to understand, Paris walks us past ancient shelves made of wood with elegantly handwritten signs on their darkly stained ends. The giant book simply floats beside her.

My gaze falls randomly on various leather-bound volumes. "Witch Wars?"

The ghost across the way shushes me from his shadowy nook.

"Sorry," I mouth.

Paris' helper, the apparition she refers to as Mee-maw Iula, keeps smiling as she levitates next to me. It denotes that she knows a secret. I see Paris in her features and assume Mee-maw stands for grandmother. Iula glides along with her hands lifted, as if in a state of constant surprise or possibly readiness. For what, I don't know.

Paris directs me to a scarred oak table and the book plops on it, the weight making it shake. Dust flies. "Every witch in each county in Georgia has a history documented by us. Normally, the Magical Library of Witches and Wizards is tended to by my sister, London, but she's off to North Carolina on business. The name of the witch in question?"

I frown, not knowing if she means the one in the necklace or the woman who cursed her into it.

Iula rubs her fingers and thumbs together in anticipation. "Either is fine, dear."

So, grandma reads minds? I clamp down on my thoughts, imagining some of Winter's energy forming a bubble around me. "The witch in the necklace is Cocheta Bonham."

Iula wags a single finger back and forth. "Not *Co*-cheta. The name is Creek. They pronounce it *Shosheta*."

"O-*kay*."

Paris frowns. "Cocheta Bonham Reynaud?"

I shrug. "My friend only said Bonham. Why?"

The ghost at the table makes a loud *shushing* noise and glares over his glasses at us.

Paris and Iula ignore him, exchanging a fearful look with each other. "The Grave Digger," Paris whispers.

Iula wrings her hands. "Oh dear."

The blood drains from my face at their reaction. My fingers feel like ice, the temperature in the basement seeming to drop twenty degrees. "Who's that?"

Iula tries to cover her anxiety with a smile. "That's her nickname."

The book flies open on its own accord, the cover smacking on the table before tea-stained colored pages flip in quick succession. No one's touching it, and startled, I take a step back.

My eyes catch snippets as they fly by—designations of covens, historical events, and then what appears to be a White Pages listing of hundreds and hundreds of names.

When they come to a stop, Paris runs a finger along a line of flamboyant handwriting, finding an entry with a garble of letters and numbers. "Cocheta was well known in this area and has an entire book dedicated to her...achievements."

She rattles off the call number and Iula disappears down a long aisle of bookshelves.

I swallow hard. "Do I want to know why she's called that?"

As if it's not obvious.

Paris' smile is jerky as she tries to reassure me and fails. "Like I said, she was—and still is— quite famous among the magickal societies in this area." She waves a hand over the book and the pages flip more leisurely this time. "And the witch who cursed her? Do you happen to know her name?"

"If Cocheta is so famous, how come you don't know what happened?"

Paris stiffens, but her smile stays in place. Patience must be one of her virtues. "As I mentioned, London is the expert on magickal societies. Everyone's heard of the Grave Digger, but I don't remember the circumstances around her death. That was a long time ago."

Haunted libraries, magickal societies. My brain is starting to cramp. "Birdie-Bell Dupree Fleming is the woman who supposedly cursed Cocheta's spirit into the necklace, but I doubt you'll locate her in there."

Paris finds what she's looking for and takes off for the stacks. "We'll see."

Iula returns with a large, leather-bound volume, almost the same as the one on the table. As previously, this one floats along beside her and lands next to the other. The title reads Cocheta's name with a few more surnames thrown in.

A biography?

The reference book opens on its own and Iula begins reading. "Cocheta was an initiate of Voodoo queen Marie Laveau and was reputed to be a great healer, fortune teller, herbalist, and midwife."

Herbalist and midwife... "That's what they labeled my great-grandmother, Tabitha. Is that some kind of code for witch?"

Iula offers a contained smile as answer.

"Why is Cocheta nicknamed the Grave Digger?"

Several pages move on their own, stopping on a section titled, "The Hollow Hills."

Iula taps the page, her spectral finger seeming to go right through it. "The white man was moving into this area at that time by the hundreds. The government wasn't respectful and the Creek were being pushed out, killed, and deceived. Cocheta was a steward of her family and that line extended to at least fifty members in the local area.

"A dozen, including Cocheta's son, were killed on All Hallows' Eve by vigilantes who wanted the Creek to leave. The next full moon, she invited those same men to a hill north of town, promising to turn over the land to them."

Iula gives me a quick glance before continuing. "They were

all found dead come morning, and because it was feared the bodies were cursed, they were buried there, exactly where they'd fallen. Cocheta claimed she never made it to the hill that night and there was no proof of her involvement, but…"

At least some of this lines up with the story Helen told me. An eye for an eye—or in this case, a son for a son.

There's a lump the size of a peach pit lodged in my throat. "How could Birdie-Bell take on this gal and live to tell about it?"

Paris returns with numerous books and spreads them out. Each flips to specific entries. "Because Elizabeth 'Birdie-Bell' Dupree Fleming was no stranger to magick."

"She was a witch?"

"In some ways, yes. She was the daughter of famed knock-em down, circuit preacher and healer, Brother Billie Dupree."

Chapter Eleven

They both eye me as if this should mean something to me. "I'm sorry, who's this guy?"

"A magician!" Iula exclaims. "Crowds followed him and his family everywhere they went. Several towns on his circuit offered him free housing if he would stay and preach full time."

"He was a preacher *and* a magician? As in stage magic?"

Paris snickers.

Iula is excited. "He'd be preaching and all of a sudden half the crowd would up and faint, claiming to be overtaken by the Spirit."

"You were around then?"

She gives me a wink from behind her glasses. "I never saw him in person, but it was rumored among certain circles that he had a powder he threw over the crowd to enchant them."

"Wait, was it real sorcery or just tricks?"

"Both, Avalon, and he taught Birdie everything he knew. Used her in his act some days."

"Ahh, okay. I get it. He was a showman."

"Exactly!" Her fingers flutter in the air. "A little hexing, a little hoaxing. But the truth is, they both had real power in their veins."

The apparition with the goatee clears his throat and Iula waves a hand at him as if he's an annoying fly. She skims a passage. "Birdie was a grown woman by the time her altercation with Cocheta occurred. Had her own family. She'd no doubt expanded her powers and wasn't afraid of going head-to-head with her."

Paris uses a finger to check paragraphs in a different book, and stops on a spot that she taps. "Says here Birdie and her husband won land in an auction the state of Georgia held, and it was lived on by a Creek family."

Iula flutters her upheld fingers again, slower this time. "Cocheta's?"

Paris nods and continues. "Cocheta's family home was burned down twice. Birdie's cows wouldn't produce milk and their well went sour. There are several other misfortunes listed, too."

I lean on the table, glancing at the information. "They kept cursing each other?"

As the three of us continue reading, I don't know whether to feel relieved or more worried. I'm not sure how any of this helps me, but it's fascinating.

"What I need to know is, how do I break this last curse Birdie put on Cocheta? How do I get Cocheta's ghost to move on and leave my boyfriend alone?"

The women look at me with blank expressions.

"Don't get me wrong, I'm grateful for all this information," I reassure them, "but it doesn't actually assist me with my problem."

Their dual attentions return to the volumes, both frowning. For long moments, I watch as they browse more passages, flip pages, and read as fast as they can.

Iula's glasses sparkle in the low light, or maybe my eyes are playing tricks on me, when she finally returns her gaze to mine. "I'm afraid none of our books are what you need for this."

"Then what do I need?"

Paris gives me a sympathetic look. "A knock-em down preacher with a gift of magick."

Chapter Twelve

T he ghost in the corner sucks in an audible breath, and I turn to find him eavesdropping on our conversation. Is he actually drawing air into his incorporeal lungs?

My stress level is so high, I feel as though I could scream. We haven't exactly been quiet, but I'm still annoyed. Not just by him, but by all of this. My head starts to pound and my stomach churns. "Mind your own business," I say rather rudely over my shoulder.

He quirks a brow and returns to his reading. I twist back to the two librarians. "How is a preacher going to help me?"

"Not simply any preacher," Iula states. "A very specific one."

Paris thumbs through pages and runs a finger under words as she reads aloud. "Birdie used her father's secret powder to hold and contain the spirits of those who had crossed her family, in order to take their magick from them. By trapping them, she could hold them hostage and keep drawing on their sorcery to enchant people."

"Great," I say, throwing my hands up. "She was a real peach. I'm guessing it only works for two centuries, right? I get that.

She's been dead a long time, so she's not drawing on anyone's sorcery anymore, is she?"

"It's possible she's still attached to Cocheta and using her power from the other side."

"That's just...wrong." I rub my temples. "How does knowing all this help me?"

Paris flicks her gaze to me, back to the book. "You need a preacher like her father to enchant the spirit."

I repeat the information to make sure I'm getting it. "A knock-em down preacher who can enchant Cocheta's spirit?"

A nod.

"To do what? Cross over?"

Another nod. "That would be ideal."

Iula taps a finger to her jaw. "The Duprees and the Flemings became successful land owners and acquired as much as they could get their hands on. It's possible they used magick to do it. Both families are still some of the wealthiest in the state."

Paris, whispering once more, looks fearful. "I don't think it's only your boyfriend you have to worry about if Cocheta gets loose."

"What do you mean? My client specifically said Cocheta will come after Logan."

Iula nods at Paris in agreement before she speaks to me. "All of the blood relatives, along with those who've married into the family, are in danger."

"Lovely. This day keeps getting better and better." I flop into a chair. "How do I find a knock-em-down Methodist preacher with enchantment powder capable *and* willing to take on a hex and an angry ghost?"

Mr. Goatee clears his throat once more.

I glance over, my voice bitter. "Get over yourself already. I have real problems here! Keep pushing it and I'll cross you over and you'll have to read in heaven."

The next thing I know, he's floating at my elbow.

"Ack!" I jump. "Dude, not cool."

"I would extend my services." Holding out a hand, he gives me a semi-bow. His vintage suit, complete with a pocket watch attached to his vest by a chain, and his bifocals, give him an air of intelligence and good taste. A tip of his head and he places a deer-stalker hat on it, looking all the world like my idea of Sherlock Holmes.

My cell buzzes and I hold up a finger. "I'm not sure I need your kind of assistance." Whatever that may be.

Caller ID shows Mama, and I see I've already missed three texts from Logan, Daddy, and Rosie, and another call from her.

Service down here must be terrible. I click on the button and say, "Mama, can I get back to you? I'm in the middle of something important."

"Where are you, Ava?" She's crying.

I move several steps from the group. "I had to run an errand. What's wrong?"

"It's Sean." Her voice hitches. "He's dead!"

Chapter Thirteen

※⚘※

Not only is Sean dead, his body was discovered in a very interesting, and quite public place...my front lawn.

Evening hangs like mist around the group on the sidewalk in front of The Wedding Chapel. Red and blue police lights blink through the descending darkness.

The porch light is on and a spotlight on a squad car illuminates the sleigh and Christmas decorations.

It also casts a bright beam on Sean's lifeless body.

I have to park across the street in front of Logan's office, since there's no spot left at my place. I nearly forget to take the bag from Chicks with Gifts Emporium, my attention riveted on the mayhem. Tabby meows and paws the bag, one nail tearing through the paper. I grab both her and the bag, and together we make our way to the sidewalk where people have gathered.

Detective Jones, a former beat cop when my dad was chief here, stands with feet planted next to the coroner. The two men speak in hushed tones and the latter points at Sean's body. An ambulance is present, although no lights flash from it, along with several people dressed in dark lab coats milling around.

They're wearing vests that state they're crime scene investigators, and they are quite serious as they place yellow numbers around the body and snap pictures.

As I stare at Sean, my legs go weak. The cool night air sticks to my skin, making me shiver. Whatever happened to him, it was no accident.

Logan is on the sidewalk near the street, leaning on the gate. Mama, Daddy, Rosie, and a gathering of neighbors surround him. Rhys watches from the front of the bed and breakfast, his eyes wide when they meet mine across our joined yards.

The EMTs lift Sean onto a gurney, and the coroner nods at something the detective says before motioning for them to wait to zip the body bag. Jones scrutinizes those of us at the gate, Mama holding out her arms to me and offering a hug as I join them.

"What happened?" I set Tabby down and she sidles up to Dad, rubbing his pant leg.

"No one knows." Rosie draws her jacket tighter against the breeze. "I was getting ready to leave and saw him through the trees just... lying out here on the ground. I might have missed him if it weren't for the Christmas lights."

Mama sobs softly. "How could this happen? What was he doing here?"

Logan rubs my arm as we all look at Dad. He picks up Tabby and she purrs, rubbing her head under his chin. His forehead is puckered in a frown, and he shrugs. "I was upstairs taking a nap. He didn't say anything about stopping by when I saw him at lunch."

"You had lunch with him?" Mama nearly screeches. All heads turn toward us.

Detective Jones steps over and points at Dad. "Would you mind stepping closer, please?"

Dad gives me a worried look then does as requested. The

squeak of the gate grates on my nerves. He places Tabby inside the fence and follows his former coworker a few feet from us.

Logan puts an arm around my waist, and Mama holds my hand, the bag rustling between us. Her sobbing grows as she stares at the body, and I wonder how close they've grown over the past few weeks.

There's a vindictive part of me that wants to tell her about his girlfriend, and I scan the crowd looking for the woman Rhys told me about. Even if she's here, I probably wouldn't recognize her, and if she was, wouldn't she come forward?

My sense of dread grows as Dad's face flashes through concern and denial. Then his features morph into something I've rarely seen—fear.

I can't stand it any longer. I throw open the gate, break from Logan and Mama's grips, and march up to the detective. "What is it? What's going on?"

Jones gives me a disapproving look. "Miss Ava, please wait outside until I'm finished interrogating your father."

"Interrogating?" My voice has taken on the pitch of my mother's earlier outburst. The crowd's murmuring now falls silent again. My stomach feels sick as I glance at all the eyes on me, at the too bright light illuminating the front yard.

As if he's already dismissed me, Jones motions for Dad to follow him to Sean's body.

"This is my property," I remind him.

He pays no attention to me, nor does he answer my questions.

I hate to admit it, but I have a sixth sense about where this is going, and it is scaring the bejesus right out of me. "Whatever it is," I murmur to Dad, "don't say anything."

He takes my hand and squeezes it. "You really should do as he says," he whispers.

Jones clears his throat from next to the gurney. I tug Dad into the shadows, ignoring the detective's glare. Lowering my voice as well, I scan my father's shadowed features. "What did he say to you? Why do you look gray right now?"

The wind kicks up hard, lifting my hair. A fresh chill trickles down my spine as he squeezes again. "Everything will be okay, I promise. The most important thing is that you know I love you."

If this is supposed to make me feel better, it doesn't. I see that fear in his eyes once more when the spotlight beam catches in them.

"Daddy, what's going on? Please tell me."

"Nash," Jones calls. Still glaring at me, he crooks a single finger at Dad. Dad tries to move away, but I keep my grip on him and move with him, shooting Jones a full-on glare Aunt Willa would be proud of. I want him to know I'm not leaving my father alone to face him.

We stop beside the gurney and I keep my eyes pinned on the detective, avoiding looking at Sean's bleak face. The coroner whistles softly under his breath, as if this an everyday occurrence. He checks his watch, signifying he's already dreaming about dinner and bed.

"You're certain you had nothing to do with Sean O'Reilly's death?" Jones says.

Dad gives an exasperated shake of his head. "Come on, Landon. You know me. We worked together for years. I would never hurt anybody."

Jones puts his hands on his belt buckle, looking all the world like a big city police officer chasing down his prey with skill. "Evidence says differently."

"What evidence?" I demand. My voice echoes across the lawn.

From behind me, Mama calls my name. I wave her off.

With a gloved hand, the coroner carefully takes Sean's chin and forces the man's mouth open. "It appears the victim may have choked to death. I can't make an official cause yet, but I did find something lodged in his throat."

Jones points inside Sean's mouth with a penlight. "The doctor got a grip on it, pulled it out. Take a look and tell me what you see."

Dad and I lean closer, peering into the space. Another chill races down my spine when I recognize what's lying on Sean's tongue.

"What is it?" Mama calls.

"Oh Daddy," I murmur, heart sinking.

Dad straightens and rubs a hand over his face. "Landon, I'm telling you, I had nothing to do with this."

Detective Jones scans the yard and crowd, then lowers his voice as he pressures Dad with his confident gaze. "Then why was your guitar pick shoved down this man's throat?"

Chapter Fourteen

✵

"**M**aybe he tripped and choked on it accidentally," I theorize. At the same time, I scan for Sean's ghost, or the one attached to him the previous night. "Did anybody see my father choke the poor guy? Of course not. You're jumping to horrible conclusions!"

No apparitions appear, and I'm unsure whether I should be glad or disappointed. I eye the silent cat gargoyles on the porch railings, along with the matching door knocker—all of whom are usually quite talkative and love to tattle on people.

Deathly silence meets my ears, all three inanimate and quiet.

Detective Jones does not appreciate my opinion, as evidenced by his tone. "There are no witnesses...yet."

"So, you're conjecturing that my dad not only shoved that down Sean's throat, but that he did it on my front lawn, out in public, and left an obvious calling card to the crime?" I lean in and glare at the detective. "You know in this town that would never work. Someone would see the perpetrator."

Jones scowls. The corner of Dad's mouth quirks. "She's got you there, Landon."

"This was no accident," he argues.

"If it's a homicide, someone is framing my father for it, and doing a poor job at that."

Jones shifts his focus to Dad. "I have to cover every angle, and things don't look good for you, Nash."

I throw my hands up, exasperated. "He didn't do it!"

Dad grabs my arms and ushers me a few feet away. "It's okay, Ava. I know how to handle this."

The next few minutes go by in a blur. Jones compels my father into his squad car to take him to the station for a formal statement. Logan plants a kiss on my forehead and tells me not to worry. He dashes across the street to jump in his Porsche and follow them.

The coroner loads the body into his van; the EMTs leave at the same time.

The excitement over, the gathered crowd disperses like a slow leaking faucet. A few wave and nod before wandering off. Others side-eye us and converse in hushed gossip as they fade into the shadows of other homes.

Mama is devastated. Rosie and I escort her around the cordoned off scene and get her inside. She cries softly, sitting at my kitchen table, and I think about all she's lost lately. Rosie places her tote with Fern in it at her desk, then fills the kettle with water. I rummage in the cupboard for teabags. Tabby saunters in, sniffs at Mama, and bails.

The doorbell rings and Rosie and I exchange a glance. "I'll see who it is," she says.

As I settle on a chamomile and lemon balm blend, I hear her heave an annoyed sigh. "I don't believe this."

Leaving the box of tea open on the counter, I lean to see who it is.

Thornhollow's only two reporters have arrived. One is on the porch, trying to talk Rosie into opening the door. A flash of light behind him illuminates the other who is snapping pictures of the lawn, the yellow tape, and the Christmas display.

Through the glass, Rosie gives our visitor a piece of her mind. He argues that he knows Dad is in town, that he and Sean had words over Mama. He wants a quote for the morning paper.

Words over Mama? At lunch?

I sink into the door frame as the reporter rattles on, wondering if my father has inadvertently sealed his own fate.

We don't have a blind to pull down, and I make a mental note to get one. Even as Rosie stomps away, he keeps tapping his pen on the glass and yelling questions at her.

The kettle whistles. At the stove, I switch it off and Rosie returns, mumbling under her breath about manners. She stands next to me as I pour the water in the cup and hisses, "Can you believe the audacity?"

"They're reporters." I dunk the bag up and down in the steaming liquid, letting the scent calm my nerves. "Takes a lot to do their job in a small town like this."

"Did you hear what he was saying?" Her dark eyes are livid. "About two murders in three months and both having ties to you and your family? It was as if you personally have something to do with all of this!"

Mama sobs louder and I add an ice cube to cool the drink. It gives me a moment to decide how to respond, because in all honesty, the reporter is right—Thornhollow is no big city and crime is rare. I don't know when the last murder occurred, but I'm guessing long before I was born.

I set the cup on the table and motion for Mama to drink. The tapping has quit and I peak to see the reporters have left. Probably headed to the station to see if they can get Jones to give them something for the record. "Go home, Rosie. It's late and there's nothing else you can do."

"Are you sure?" She rubs my back. "I can stay if you want. I don't mind."

A few more reassurances and she and Fern leave.

I pace as Mama plays with her cup. She doesn't look up when she says, "Sean and your Dad fought all the time."

I stop and lean on the counter, my stomach twisting. "About what?"

She runs a finger around the rim, takes a sip. "Do you think your Dad could be jealous of Sean? Enough to...you know."

I grip my hands together, feeling the urge to strangle her. I need to get out to the front porch and question the gargoyles. "Daddy did *not* kill him, Mama. I can't believe you would think that."

"I don't," she admits. Her shoulders shake as she begins crying again. "But it does look bad, Ava. What are we going to do?"

I tap my fingers, watching Arthur and Lancelot stroll in. They roam in search of food, giving Mama a wide berth. They're not whining like normal, as if sensing something's wrong, but I probably should feed the poor cats anyway.

In the pantry, I pull out the dry food, then shake some into each of their bowls as well as Tabitha's. She appears in a cloud of fluff and all three descend on it with gusto. Their dinner is gone in seconds.

"We don't know for sure he was killed," I state. "Detective Jones might know what he's doing, but there could be various reasons Sean died on the front lawn."

Mama glances up with equal amounts of hope and disbelief. "An accident?"

I return the bag to the pantry and close the door, watching the cats clean their faces. "It's possible."

"What about the guitar pick?"

"I don't know why he had one of Dad's business cards in his mouth, but maybe he was chewing on it. Like a nervous habit or something. Remember when I would do that to pencil erasers in fifth grade? Drove you nuts."

She nods, taking another sip.

"Did you by chance ever see him chewing on random things like that?"

Her cup claps on the table as she sets it down, face scrunching in determination. "Not that I recall. He took a lot of antacids. Said his stomach was a mess."

That can happen when you live on alcohol. "He could have tripped and fell and it went down his throat."

The hope in Mama's eyes fades. "I suppose that's one possibility." She shrugs. "It's pretty weak, though."

"Well, if he was murdered, it wasn't Daddy, and we'll figure out who's framing him for it."

Queenie arrives, blustering past me when I open the door and heading straight for Mama. It's like she has radar and the two friends share a long hug.

At the same time, the ghost from the library materializes near the mudroom. The cats jump but the women don't notice.

"Interesting," he says, eyeing the decor and floating past us, out of the kitchen, and vanishing up the stairs.

"Don't you worry," Queenie insists to Mama. "Not for one minute. Everything's gonna work out fine."

I'm reminded of what my father said to me. *"Everything's going to be okay, sweetie. The most important thing is that you know I love you."*

It's not reassuring.

Still holding onto my mother, Queenie looks me over. "Your Daddy got a lawyer?"

I nod. "Logan."

"Good. I'm gonna take your Mama home, put her to bed. You okay?"

"Sure, I'm fine," I lie.

I see the two out, wait until they've disappeared and question the inanimate felines on the porch.

"You saw what happened. Tell me."

Gold eyes turn to me. "He wasn't killed," the door knocker says.

"But he's dead. Did he choke on the pick accidentally?"

"It was no accident," one of the porch cats purrs.

"How is that possible?"

The matching gargoyle yawns. "Humans are so dense."

"My dad could be in serious danger," I tell them. "If you can shed light on what happened, please do so."

"Your dad is innocent," Door knocker states.

"I'm aware of that. Who's guilty?"

"No one," the twin gargoyles sing-song.

They talk in circles for another minute and I give up.

Inside, the bag with the hex box and the other items sits forgotten on the kitchen counter. I toy with it and wonder if I'm the one who's cursed.

Chapter Fifteen

❧❦❧

When I search the cabinets for Aunt Willa's secret stash of brandy, I come up empty, but Rhys arrives, letting himself in through the mudroom door.

He hugs me tight and sets me back a foot. "You look like death warmed over."

The ghost drifts past the open doorway. I want to question him about what he's doing here, see if he can find out if Sean's around, but Brax arrives on Rhys' heels.

I pull out the opened wine bottle from the previous night as I recite what I know. Brax rolls his eyes at the wine and goes straight to the high cabinet above the fridge. There he removes the brandy. We sit at the table, discussing the incident, and the warm liquor and their company helps calm my nerves.

"Tell me about Haylee Dean Bower," I say. "Any idea where she was earlier this evening?"

Both men give me an odd look.

I raise my hands in a 'what' gesture.

"The Toad at one point," Rhys says, "but I don't remember the exact time. Why?"

"You told me she was Sean's girlfriend. He was also dating my mother. A woman scorned, seeking revenge, and who knows…?"

They glance at each other. Brax refills my glass. "I just came from there and didn't see her."

I don't drink the second shot, shoving it back. "I'm gonna find and question her."

Rhys plants his hands on the table and rises. "I'll drive. You've had a rough day, and we all know you and brandy don't mix."

"I'm fine."

I am, too.

"I'm still going with you," he insists.

Brax apologizes that he can't. He needs to return to work. Not only do the partners own the Thorny Toad and the B&B, Brax has a coffee bar next to his mama's diner that serves alcohol in the evenings.

He kisses my cheek and I hug him before he leaves.

"When's the last time you ate?" Rhys asks.

"I can't remember."

"No wonder you're so peaked." He opens the fridge and withdraws the box of leftover pizza. "Perfect. I love Vinnie's."

He puts a slice on a plate and pours me a glass of sweet tea. "Eat."

"I can't."

Grabbing a scratchpad and pen from the junk drawer, he sits across from me. "Yes, you can. Let's make a list of people to talk to if we can't find her. We need a plan."

He's right. I'm about to bite into my slice when Persephone pops in. The angelic guardian angel may be a bigger pain in my backside than the cat.

Tonight, she appears in a rainbow handkerchief dress, a large sapphire ring on her index finger, and her hair done in a cascade of braids. I'm not sure what fashion statement she's going for, but it almost hurts to look at it.

At least with her, I can have a conversation, and she's been helpful with previous issues. "Where have you been?"

She lifts a single brow and sniffs at the food. "You're not my only charge, you know."

"I'm in real trouble here and I've been trying to reach you."

Rhys' head swivels to the place I'm glaring at. He can't see her, but he knows about my abilities and accepts them. "Is it that gal who dresses like Endora from *Bewitched?*"

That is the fashion statement Persephone prefers. I nod. "I could use some insight," I say to her. "I have a lot of questions that need answering."

She gives me an impatient look but before she can respond, Sherlock materializes next to her.

She startles, and he, too, looks surprised. He adjusts his spectacles to take her in. "Madam."

Her eyes shoot daggers at me. "Who is this?"

From what I've learned, guardian angels don't know everything. "Never mind about him. Are you here to help me or not?"

She crosses her arms over her chest. "You picked up a ghost hitchhiker?"

"Well, it's not like you were hanging around, protecting me from him."

"I'm a crack detective," Sherlock states, looking down his nose at her, "and have offered my services to young Ava."

"I bet you have." Her mouth screws up and she taps a finger against her arm. "You know I can't give you answers to certain questions," she relents to me, "but I'll do what I can to point you in the right direction."

It's the best I can get from her, and I'm desperate enough that I'll take it.

I tell Rhys about her, Sherlock, the necklace in the box, and eat all at the same time.

Persephone and Sherlock dance around each other, like a couple of dogs sniffing their territory. Persephone grows interested in the hex box as I show it to Rhys. "This is probably the biggest thing I have to deal with and I'm running out of time, but tonight, I have to figure out how to help Dad."

All three nod their understanding. Rhys watches as I return the box to the bag. "We should start with Reverend Stout. Maybe he can tell us where to find Haylee, and I know if Brax sees her he'll text and let us know where she is."

I gather my coat and purse, eye the last shot of brandy but resist.

Outside, Rhys hops in the passenger seat of my car. Tabby, Persephone, and Sherlock climb in back.

Reverend Stout's home is a beautiful old Victorian. The doorbell makes a resounding *bing bong* when we arrive.

The Reverend and his wife have modest holiday decorations, mostly focused on the birth of Jesus. Removing the reading glasses from the end of his nose, he appears mildly surprised to see Rhys and I standing on his front porch. "Ava, Rhys, to what do I owe this pleasure?"

He's in sweatpants and a cheerful red and green sweater. Usually, he's in a black suit, or, when on the ambulance crew— his second job—a white shirt and blue pants.

I'm not sure I've ever seen him in such casual attire. "We're so sorry to bother you this evening, but we're looking for your niece, Haylee Dean."

He motions us to step inside and we do, Rhys closing the door behind us. "Does this have something to do with Sean O'Reilly's death?"

He's already heard. The news must be all over town by now. "I understand she and Sean have been seeing each other."

He uses his glasses to point to a room on the right. "Why don't you come on in?"

Rhys and I follow him into a quaint den with stacks of books on the table. One lies open waiting for him to return to it. A gorgeous Tiffany-style lamp makes the room glow, and I see touches of his wife's personality throughout. She loves to knit and do other crafts, and there are doilies on every upholstered surface, a knitted Afghan on the couch. Pictures of them from their married life rest on a nearby table, and she has a macramé pot hanger in a corner with a philodendron. The big leaves cascade to the floor.

There's a discreet Christmas tree opposite the sofa, and I see handmade ornaments on it. They make me smile.

"I'm afraid I don't have a close relationship with her," he tells us. "My sister's kid. Haylee was always a rebel, much like her mother. When she got old enough, she traveled a lot, hung out with bands and did something the kids call couch surfing, I think? Never had a close relationship with our Lord."

"Is it possible she was a groupie for my Dad's band?"

He toys with the glasses. "She played percussion in high school and believed she was meant to be a country star. Wrote her own songs, tried recording a few." He looks wistfully at the table with the family pictures arranged on it. "When she graduated, she took off for Nashville, said she'd never set foot in this town again. She ended up back here about three months later, and eventually persuaded your father to let her in his band. I believe it had something to do with Sean. She fell pretty hard for him."

This is news to me and I sit back. "Haylee played in Dad's band back in the day?"

"I try not to speak ill of folks, but I believe Sean preyed on her need to be a famous singer. I also think Nash felt sorry for her and created a spot for her." He winks at me. "Nice guy, your dad."

He crosses his legs and taps his glasses on one knee. "Things didn't go well, and Nash kicked her out because she wasn't reliable. Mr. O'Reilly left town shortly after, if memory serves."

Mrs. Stout bustles in, all southern grace covering her surprise. "Why, my, my. I heard the doorbell and look who's popped in for a visit."

She offers herbal tea or decaf coffee. Rhys and I thank her but pass. "We'll be done shortly and leave you two be," I tell her.

"The reverend does have an appointment in a few minutes," she says, with a deft smile. "A scheduled meeting."

Her very gracious way of saying our unscheduled visit needs to wrap up.

"I'll finish with Ava and Rhys and get ready for it in a moment," her husband says.

Once she leaves, I resume. "Have you seen her since she's been in town for the holidays?"

He shakes his head. "I'm sorry I can't be of more help, but we don't have that type of bond. Her mother died while she was on the road with the band. I miss my sister greatly, but neither she nor her daughter value family like we do."

As Rhys and I are leaving, Penn and Beau John Reed show up. We greet each other and Penn promises she'll pay her late bill as soon as she can. I think about the fact we're all struggling in our own ways, and I reassure her that it's okay, I know she's good for it. She doesn't even know that I delivered a message from her grandmother to her at her wedding. I'm pleased to see the late Mrs. Calhoun is no longer hanging around in Penn's aura.

Persephone floats next to my ear as Rhys and I descend the steps, her voice startling me. "You might ask that gal if she's seen this Haylee character."

Clearing my throat, I stop and pivot. "Penn? Any chance you know Haylee Dean Bower?"

She glances at Stout, then nods at me. "I saw her earlier today."

"Where was she?"

"Walking past your place. I was on my way to work and saw her standing outside the gate."

The gargoyles definitely didn't mention this. "What was she doing?"

"Just staring at the house. For a minute, I wondered if she was gettin' married, the way she peered at the window displays."

Rhys grips the railing. "Did she enter the property?"

Suspicious now, Penn's face turns serious. "I was driving by and not paying a lot of attention. Why?"

"'Cuz of that O'Reilly guy," Beau tells her. "Right?" he asks of me. His accent is heavy. "They was a thing, from what I heard."

"Eww," Penn comments. "Kinda old for her, wasn't he?"

"Thank you," I say. "Sorry to keep you."

Rhys and I walk to the car. Persephone is nowhere to be seen but Sherlock is waiting in the back. He stares at the couple entering the house. "Is this the man we need to help us with the hex?"

"You tell me. He's not Methodist, and I've never seen him knock people out with his preaching."

"Ah, well, I assume he won't do then."

As I reverse out of the space, I glance at him. "You don't really believe you're Sherlock Holmes, do you?"

He feigns resentment. "I certainly am."

"Where's your British accent?"

Persephone pops in next to him and twitches her lips. "She's got you there, buster."

Sherlock vanishes. Persephone shrugs and disappears as well.

It's like ghostly tag in the backseat.

Rhys gets a text from Brax. *No dice at the Toad.*

Driving aimlessly, hoping to spot Haylee, I review the possibilities. Thornhollow isn't that big.

My phone rings and I hurriedly pull to the curb, seeing who it is. "Daddy?"

"Hey, where are you? I got home and the place is dark."

"You're out?"

"Of course, I am. Circumstantial evidence is all Jones has. The coroner will perform the autopsy and the police have interviews to do. They'll figure out what happened."

"What a relief! They better leave you alone."

"Hey, your boyfriend's here. Looks like you left in a hurry. Willa's best brandy is on the table. Where'd you go?"

"I'm heading home right now."

"Ava, sweetie. Don't worry, all right?"

I yank the wheel to change direction, once again feeling some hope. "Just don't drink all the brandy before I get there."

Chapter Sixteen

By the time I return, Daddy's in bed, and I'm disappointed.

Logan is waiting with hot chocolate, complete with tiny marshmallows and a candy cane. "Said he was exhausted and he'd talk to you tomorrow."

We take our seats in front of the fireplace, and I'm itching to check my messages. While I was looking for Haylee, Winter called, as did an unknown number—my intuition tells me that one is Paris.

Well, my intuition and Sherlock. Hovering in the living room, he tries to get me to hurry Logan along so I can get back to the business at hand.

Logan's argyle socked feet are on the coffee table, and he wears a serious expression on his face as he watches the flames in the hearth. They dance, throwing golden light over his features.

I nudge him. "What is it? What aren't you telling me?"

He glances toward the staircase and lowers his voice. "I don't want you to worry, but I have a feeling someone is setting up your dad."

"That's exactly what I think. I suspect Haylee Dean Bower is involved." I relate what Penn told me. "I haven't tracked her down yet, but when I do, I'll get to the bottom of this."

He doesn't seem convinced. "She has to be staying here in town. Somebody must know where she's at."

"Are you up for helping me make a few calls?"

We set our cocoas down and take out our phones. In twenty minutes, we have no further leads, and it's late enough that people are starting to get annoyed at the invasion. I've put Rosie and Queenie on the hunt, though, so I know we'll track her down soon enough.

I finish my drink, torn between savoring this peaceful moment and sending Logan off with a kiss so I can return to the other issues, especially the one concerning him.

He rubs my back, takes the empty cup from my hand, and rises. "You need rest, and I've got a big day tomorrow."

I trail after him to the kitchen. He rinses the mugs and puts them in the dishwasher as I soak up every inch of him and consider telling him the truth. He hugs and kisses me before he leaves, and I hold my tongue.

As he crosses the street to his place, I stare at the vulgar yellow police tape trembling in the breeze. I confront the cat door knob. "You didn't tell me Haylee Dean Bower was here."

"Don't know who that is," the cat answers with a sleepy yawn.

"You didn't see her attack Sean?"

"No one attacked him," one of the gargoyles snarls. "Go to bed!"

I turn off the porch light and head upstairs. They aren't ones to lie. At least I have no reason to believe so, but if it's not an accident and no one killed Sean...that would mean it was natural causes.

"He tripped and choked," I tell myself again.

But the idea of Haylee knocking him off still clings to my mind.

In order not to wake my father, I text Winter after listening to her voicemail and let her know I've collected the ingredients for the spells. They and the hex box sit on the dresser.

I fill her in about the preacher and also mention I might be able to get help from Raven's sister. I'll feel more confident if she's here to guide me. Winter replies, wishing me luck, and insisting I keep her in the loop.

As expected, Paris left me the name and number of two different preachers who may be able to assist in reversing Birdie's hex. I take down the information, knowing it's too late to call them right now. *First thing tomorrow.*

I reach out to contact Sherlock to share the news. He doesn't respond to my summons, and I wonder if he's as unreliable as Persephone.

Ghosts. They don't adhere to time and space limitations and can be exceptionally erratic, vague, and frustrating.

I can't sleep, tossing and turning all night. The cats usually camp on the bed with me, but they abandon it and find more peaceful lodgings.

The next morning, I trail after the smell of coffee and discover Daddy making breakfast. He's already eaten, and as I enjoy the biscuits and eggs, he plays snippets of a new song he's working on, filling the kitchen with the sound of his guitar and voice. I enjoy every minute of it, putting off the impending awkward conversations I'm due to have today.

"Brax and Rhys are having an open house this afternoon at the Thorny Toad," he tells me as I clean up. "I'm going to play Christmas songs."

"That's great. I'll stop by later."

Rosie arrives and shakes her head first thing, alluding to the fact she's found out nothing about Haylee. Our day kicks off with a crying bride-to-be whose mother-in-law is giving her fits about her January wedding. Dad wisely withdraws upstairs and I have to again, postpone calling preachers.

The local florist, Betty Lee, phones an hour later to tell Rosie the mistletoe has arrived for the ballroom decorations, and Rosie hustles off to pick up the boxes.

I've decided to do Winter's ritual on the locket in the attic, so when Daddy goes to the gazebo in the backyard to write lyrics, I grab the assortment of ingredients and the hex box, and carry them to the third floor. There, I try both preachers and get their voicemails. Doesn't seem like something I want to leave specifics about in a message, so I simply ask them to return my call and emphasize it's an emergency.

I rearrange old furniture and shift a wool rug out of the way to reveal the wooden slats underneath. Dust clogs my nose and makes me sneeze as I wash the stained floorboards to prepare them for my chalk drawing.

I hear Rosie return, and I return downstairs to find Dad putting on his coat and slinging his guitar case over his shoulder.

"Got to go set up." He kisses my cheek. "See you later?"

"Have fun."

None of the locals I contacted last night in my search for Haylee have returned my calls. I stifle the urge to warn him about her.

By lunch, I've reached out to more friends and acquaintances, but no one knows the woman's location. Even Queenie has failed at hunting her down. Neither preacher has responded and I try them again, with the same outcome.

Like Sherlock, it appears Haylee has vanished into thin air and perhaps these holy men have too.

My phone rings and Rhys' voice is excited when I answer. "She's here. Just arrived! What do you want me to do?"

"You're at the Toad?"

"Yep."

"Keep her there." I shove a half-eaten sandwich into the fridge and head for my coat. "I'm on my way."

The Toad is decked out for the open house, and Dad is already playing classic carols when I arrive. People filter in and out, enjoying the vendor booths and buying craft items and gifts, along with certificates for tarot readings, past life regressions, and energy healing services.

The mood is high, but as Dad plays his own holiday song, the jukebox starts up. He glares over at a woman, who's sobbing over the glowing lights of the machine. She detaches herself and ambles to the bar.

I catch Rhys' eye and he nods in her direction.

Haylee Dean.

I squeeze through the crowd. She appears quite drunk, stringy blond hair falling past her shoulders and nearly into the mug of beer in front of her. She sings with the Springsteen song on the jukebox at the top of her lungs, and I flinch at the screechy sound.

I meet Rhys at the opposite end of the bar. He wipes the counter and sets down a glass of seltzer water with a lime on the side. "She's played that song at least ten times. People are getting annoyed. If she doesn't quit, they might leave."

"So why don't you pull the plug?"

"You said to keep her here. I was afraid she'd leave if I did that."

I pat his hand. "Thank you. I'll handle this."

I mosey toward her, bringing my drink along. "I'm really sorry about Sean."

Her eyes are blurry when she lifts them to glance at me. "He was my soulmate." Her shoulders shake. "Now he's dead. What am I going to do?"

I motion at Rhys to unplug the jukebox and he does, The Boss dying in mid-chorus. Haylee doesn't even seem to notice, her nervous hands fiddling with her mug. "I wanted everything to be perfect, and then..."

"Then what?" I prompt.

She peeks from beneath her hair, and suddenly stiffens. The vacant eyes clear. "Hey, I know you."

Persephone appears next to her. "Ava, be careful."

"*Now* you show up," I murmur to the angel, and Haylee frowns.

"What?"

Persephone's tone is a warning. "Ava..."

I may be in the presence of a murderer. Combined with the fact she's drunk as a skunk, I probably should heed my angel's advice.

Haylee swivels on the seat, glaring toward Dad.

He's playing Silent Night, a handful of folks gathered to listen. Haylee flies off the bar stool, shoving a woman carrying several bags aside, as she hurls herself at him. "It should be you! You should be dead, not Sean!"

I rush after her, grabbing her an instant before she tackles him. She cries and tries to break free, but she's easy to swing around.

Dad stops playing, and I motion at him to keep going. I shove his attacker toward a booth. "Relax," I tell her as she crumples into the vinyl. "Or Rhys will throw you out."

The patrons return to their business, giving us questioning glances. I sink down across from her. "Why should my dad be dead instead of Sean?"

She clams up, so I keep prodding. "Come on, Haylee. I know you were in love with Sean, but I doubt he was your soulmate. You know he was dating others, right?"

She flops her arms on the table, head hanging, and sniffs. "He was *mine*. In his heart, he knew I was the only woman for him."

Reasoning with a drunk is not something I'm adept at. When Persephone slides in beside me, I'm almost grateful. "You better record this."

I just look at her. "Huh?"

"If you're going to get a confession, you need it for proof, and your interrogation skills could use work."

"Not helpful." But then I relent. "What do you suggest?"

"Your phone. Use it," she says, exasperated.

At the same time, Haylee lifts her head. "We had a chance, a real chance."

I fiddle with my cell, turning on the recorder app and setting it on my lap. I've never used it before and I hope it works. "At what?"

"Your daddy knew it, too," she continues, oblivious, "but he deserted us on our big night. Sean always said that was the turning point." She taps the table with a jagged fingernail. "We missed our opportunity because of him."

Dad's playing an upbeat jingle and people are enjoying it. "What do you mean deserted?"

Haylee goes silent, seemingly lost in a memory, or maybe the effects of the liquor.

Persephone reaches over and yanks a strand of her hair.

"Ouch." She glares at me, as if I'm the culprit.

"What do you mean?" I repeat.

"It was St Louis." She wipes her nose. "They sold over a thousand tickets before our debut there. It was rumored Bruce Springsteen's manager was going to be in the audience. We could have opened for him! Can you imagine it? The Boss. We would have gone big time."

I feel my father's gaze on me. He looks worried, even though he's smiling as he belts out the lyrics and the crowd sings with him. I give him a discreet wave, conveying that I'm okay, and to keep going.

"What happened?" I ask Haylee.

She snarls. "Nash said he had to get back to Thornhollow. He never even told us why, just skipped out. We couldn't take the stage without our front man."

She sits back in a huff. "All my dreams down the drain. Sean's, too. Your father ruined the band and never even told us why."

Sherlock appears next to the table and begins pacing. "Ask her what happened between her and the drummer."

Persephone nods. "Do it."

I'm slightly surprised she's agreeing with the ghost. "Did you and Sean break up then or later?"

A tear slips from the corner of Haylee's eye. "Sean went into a deep depression. Said I reminded him of the group and everything he'd lost."

"No, no, no." Sherlock is contrite, snagging his glasses from the end of his nose and waving them around. "Ask her about yesterday and the fight."

I give him a skeptical glance. "How do you know about that?"

Haylee eyes me as if I'm the one who's drunk. "What?"

Good thing she won't remember this conversation.

Sherlock jabs the glasses toward her.

Fine. "What did you and Sean fight about yesterday?"

"Fight?" She rears back. "We never fought."

"Liar," Sherlock says, replacing his spectacles. "They argued over your mother."

"What about Mama?"

I'm asking him, but Haylee's eyes widen. "Are you psychic?"

Good lord. "Did you and Sean quarrel about him seeing her? You know they had a relationship, right?"

She slides out, holding onto the table for balance. "I don't have to answer your questions."

"That's true." I set the phone on the table so she can see it. "You can talk to Detective Jones after I give him this recording of our conversation. I think he'll be interested to hear about the fight."

Outrage on her face, Haylee flings herself at me.

Chapter Seventeen

S he goes for my neck, but she's too drunk to get a firm hold. I shove her back, and she manages to throw my cell.

It clatters to the floor. "No!" Her voice cuts through the music. "I mean...you can't call him."

Nearby customers shoot looks our way once more. I rise, pick up my phone. "I don't have time to play games, Haylee. Tell me what happened or I'm going to the police."

She glances around with wild eyes. "It was nothing. Sean was..."

Sherlock looks smug, Persephone bored. "Was what? You had a fight and he ended up dead on my front lawn. I have a witness who says you were hanging around my house yesterday. Come clean with me about what happened."

She crumples back into the seat, her voice now whiny. "I wanted him back, that's all. I thought the band could reunite and he and I could start fresh." She picks at her nails. "That's why I called Greer and Huck. They're home for Christmas. It made sense. I thought lunch would be, you know, fun. We could reminisce about the old days, put some bad feelings to rest."

The band. Suddenly, I remember why Sean's ghost seemed familiar—Travis Wooten, the keyboardist who died in a motor-cycle accident.

I feel sorry for all of them. So many dreams, a lot of them gone forever.

Haylee gets some of my sympathy, too, but if she's framing my father for Sean's murder, I will stop her. I'm once again recording what she's saying, hoping for a confession. "How did that work out?"

She glares at me. "I want my Hallmark moment."

Don't we all? "Was Sean willing to get the band back together?"

She bites her bottom lip, glances over at Dad. "Sure, he just wasn't willing to get back together with me."

I slide the phone closer. "And you argued about Mama?"

Her unfocused gaze drops to the tabletop. "He didn't care one iota about her. He was using her to get at Nash."

"You followed Sean to my place, and what? Argued, things got out of hand? You killed him and made it look like my dad did it?"

Her shock seems too real to be faked. "I would never kill Sean. I love him!" A sob. "*Loved* him."

She couldn't make this easy for me, could she? I pull out one of Daddy's business cards. "Ever seen one of these?"

Her attention skitters away. "Nash has been passing them around like candy. It's like he wants to rub it in our faces that he's this big star and the rest of us are losers."

My dad is far from being as famous as she makes him out to be, but I suppose when you're stewing in bitterness over lost fame, even a little success seems cool. "Did you see Sean with one?"

As if on cue, the last strains of the song die off, and peaceful silence descends. Haylee, still speaking loudly, snickers. "He had one all right. Said he was going to make your daddy eat it, along with crow pie, before he ever forgave him for stealing our dream."

The place falls completely silent, all eyes turning to us.

"Finally, some fun," Persephone states.

Sherlock says, "Oh dear," and vanishes.

Rhys rings the bell behind the bar. "Fresh punch is ready and so are tasty snacks." He points to the refreshment table, where nothing has actually changed. "Be sure to put your name in the prize box to win a special Christmas basket!"

Again he indicates the table. He's got the attention of the patrons now so everyone stops gawking at us. He nods at Dad and my father begins playing the next song.

Haylee scoots out and stands once more. "Leave me alone. Sean was a good man, and we would've been happy together if it weren't for your family."

She staggers off toward the restroom, and I call her a cab. Then I contact Jones.

Persephone waves goodbye and dissipates into thin air.

Returning to my seltzer water at the bar, I agree to hold when the desk operator at the station answers. Rhys slides a plate with several appetizers in front of me, and I eat while I wait for the detective. When he comes on the line, he seems slightly miffed I've interrupted his day. "What is it, Fantome?"

I relay the information Haylee was in the vicinity, was upset about Sean seeing my mother, and had a vendetta against my father. "I have most of the conversation recorded, so you can listen to it."

There's a pregnant pause and a heavy sigh. "This is an official police investigation. Stop harassing people."

I take a sip. Normally, I try to be as hospitable as possible, but in this case, we're talking about my dad being framed for a murder he didn't commit. "Do you want it or not? It would look bad if I go to your superior and tell him I had potential evidence in this case that you ignored. Or maybe I'll reach out to the reporters who were at my door last night. I bet they'd love to investigate."

My straightforward confrontational attitude doesn't win him over, but he does relent. "Fine. Drop it off today at the department."

Satisfied, I click off and gobble more food.

Dad takes a break and accepts a glass of soda from Rhys. "That wasn't too embarrassing," he says to me with a smile.

I assume he's talking about Haylee's outburst and not his music. While he enjoys the holidays, I can see he'd rather be singing rock songs. "I may have a lead on Sean's death."

He steals the last appetizer from my plate. "Haylee?"

She bursts from the ladies' room, heading toward the bar. Rhys speaks to one of his waitresses, who intercepts her and directs her toward the door.

Through the front window I see the taxi I ordered pulling up. Thornhollow is so small, we don't have any actual taxis, but there's a local driver who does the Uber thing.

"Daddy, what happened the night of the St. Louis gig when you bailed on the band and came home?"

He looks askance. "Haylee told you I stood them up that night, did she?"

I nod and wait.

He shrugs and continues working on his beverage. "It was election night, and your mama thought she was going to lose to Dwight Emerson. She was in quite a panic."

I know what he's going to say before he finishes. "You gave up performing to come home and be with her during the returns, didn't you?"

He keeps his gaze on his glass. "She won. I left again in the morning."

True love. "Was Springsteen's manager really in the audience?"

Another shrug and a sad smile. "I regret nothing. It was a great moment for her, and I was happy to share it."

I'm downing another swig when my phone buzzes. It's Rosie. "How's it going?"

Her voice is an octave higher than normal. "Ava, we've got a big, big problem."

Adrenaline causes me to hop off the stool. "Now what?"

"I can't believe the supplier mixed this up!"

With the way things are going, I'd believe almost anything. "Calm down. Whatever it is, we'll figure it out and get it fixed."

Memories of toilets flooding and ruining the Country Club ballroom fill my head. It's only been two months since a ghost tried to wreck the most important wedding Thornhollow has ever seen by doing just that.

"I'm afraid we don't have time to," she tells me.

I lean over and kiss my dad on the cheek before I hustle toward the exit. "Tell me what happened."

"The boxes of mistletoe?"

I hit the door and fly down the steps, heading for my car. "What about them?"

"They didn't send the right thing, Ava. The mistletoe ball is going to need a name change."

Yep, I'm definitely cursed right now. "What did they send?"

"There won't be kissing under mistletoe this year for the big finale. I'm afraid they'll have to do it under eucalyptus."

Chapter Eighteen

I spend the afternoon hunting for mistletoe, Haylee Dean's words ringing in my ears.

The irony of Sean threatening to make my dad eat his guitar pick, then ending up dead with it lodged in his throat, isn't lost on me. While I'm running around, I email the recording to Detective Jones.

Mama calls as I'm driving to Helen's and asks what happened at the bar. Gossip is flying through town faster than Santa Claus about her, Dad, and Sean, thanks in part to the display this afternoon at the Toad. "Did you know the police told your father not to leave town?"

Her anxiety is off the charts— her voice high and tight, reminding me of Rosie, who's still at the Country Club waiting for me.

"He is a suspect, but there's nothing to worry about. Logan will get him cleared, and I'm pretty sure I know who did it."

"That woman at the bar?"

"Yes, Mama. She has means, opportunity, and motive."

"You sound like your father."

He was a cop for ten years. Guess some of that rubbed off on me. Could also be I've read too many crime novels. "At this point, Haylee is my person of interest, and I'm not done investigating yet."

"Are you sure, Ava? I remember back in the day when she was trailing after your dad and the band. I don't believe she ever had all her horses in the barn."

Mama's way of saying she's not too swift.

The mansion comes into view, and I pray I can use my leverage with Helen to talk her out of all the mistletoe she has in her house. We can't exactly have the so-named ball without the key ingredient, and we can't order more in time because it's so close to Christmas—all of the suppliers are sold out.

"Did you know she and Sean were a thing?"

My mother makes a weird noise on the other end of the line, suggesting she doesn't believe this at all. "Only in *her* mind. I'm telling you, that girl has a few screws loose."

"She told me Sean was her soulmate."

Mama laughs with derision. "They had a flirtation a long time ago, that doesn't make them soulmates."

I hate to ask the question, but I need to know. "Were you and Sean serious? You weren't…"—I make a face—"in love with him, were you?"

Please say no, please say no, please say—

"Oh, Ava. We were just having fun."

I release the breath I'm holding. It comes out in a rush. "And how do you feel about Daddy?"

"Oh dear. Sorry—I have to go. Amelia Bronson is calling about the new city administrator position. Love you!"

The line goes dead. I park, sure she has no intention of answering that question, but later I'm going to put her on the spot again. One way or another I need to know if there's any hope for reuniting my parents.

Today, Helen meets me at the door rather than her butler. "Did you do it? Did you finally get rid of that ghost?"

"I'm working on it. The reason I'm here—"

"The curse expires tomorrow!"

I bite the inside of my lower lip. "I'm aware. I need all the mistletoe in your house."

She blinks. "Will it help you save my son?"

She thinks I want the plant for a spell. I lie without hesitation this time. "I wouldn't ask otherwise."

We spend the next hour unwinding sprigs from the swags and garlands. She tries to pin me down about the specifics of how it's going to keep Logan safe, but I'm in no mood for discussing it.

"I heard about your father," she says at one point.

I'm no mood to discuss his situation with her either. "It's great to have him home for the holidays."

"I meant about the sordid business with his band member."

"Former."

"And your mother? How does she feel about all of that?"

I need to take care of the mistletoe, follow up with Detective Jones, and call Raven if I don't hear from her sister soon. Not to mention those darn preachers who still haven't called back.

I stuff some of the berry laden plant into a bag. "Mama's a rock, no matter what happens." I offer a forced smile. "I think this should be enough. Thank you."

Helen shows her disgust with my lack of insightful answers, and I try to reassure her before I go. "I'm going to work on the hex-breaking tonight, I promise. You'll be the first to know how things turn out."

As I'm driving away, praying I have enough to keep the ball from being a disaster, my phone rings. My pulse leaps as I put Jones on Bluetooth. "Well? Are you going to arrest her?"

His voice is gruff, like usual. "I still have nothing to prove she harmed Sean O'Reilly. Your interrogation is worthless."

I stomp on the brakes, nearly giving myself whiplash. "What? Come on. I have eyewitness testimony she was at my house before Sean was killed. She knew about the guitar pick and was desperate to get back with him. She blames my father for breaking up the band, and she was upset Sean was seeing my mother and didn't want to reconcile. How much more do you need?"

"I need a direct confession, and not one where you entrap the suspect. She was drunk, you were leading her, and she never admitted to anything other than being in love with him."

I beat my hand against the steering wheel. "You can't let her off the hook. She did it. I know she did."

"I suppose you looked in your crystal ball?"

Several smart retorts pass through my mind, but I decide it's unwise to say them aloud. I have to count to ten before I answer, though, letting the strained silence hang between us for a moment, before I say, "Have a nice day, officer."

Calling him that is intentional, and I don't wait for a reply. Tapping my earpiece isn't as satisfying as slamming down a handset and I throw the Bluetooth on the dash.

I sit in the middle of the road another minute, trying to decide whether proving my father's innocence or saving Logan from his family's curse is my top priority. They are equally important, and I struggle with which to address first. No clear answer comes, and neither Persephone nor Sherlock appear when I send out an SOS.

I think about Sean and the ghost I saw hanging around him that night. I try reaching out to him.

A loud *beep* jerks me from my quest. In the rearview, I see a car swerve out from around me. The driver yells and waves a fist as he goes by and I take my foot off the brake. "Merry Christmas to you, too," I mumble.

My intention is to drop off the mistletoe at the Country Club and head home, but Rosie is in such a state, I stay to help her. When I finally return to The Wedding Chapel, I find a young woman with pigtails, reflective aviator sunglasses, and a nose ring waiting for me.

I park on the street and get out. Arthur and Lancelot are in the display window behind the girl, eyeing her with a healthy amount of adoration. Tabby is nowhere to be seen, and as I open the gate and pass by the crime scene, the pigtailed woman stands, smacking the gum in her mouth. "Are you Ava?"

"I am. Can I help you?"

She hefts a large crossbody bag onto her shoulder and removes her sunglasses. Her eyes are a match for Raven's. "My sister sent me." Her fingers all have rings, and I notice a small, discreet tattoo on the left of her neck under her ear. "Said you need help with an un-hexing."

A huge weight lifts from me. "Boy, am I glad to see you."

The knocker whistles under his breath. "There's dark magick in this one. It's all over her aura. Better be careful."

As I unlock the door, I send a glance to Sage. She stops chewing a moment and grins. "Nice cat."

Great. She can hear him, too. I usher her inside.

Chapter Nineteen

✥

"Y ou've done this before?" I ask. Winter cautioned against black magick, and I'm just a wee bit worried about Sage.

She scans the interior of the house as we make our way through it. I turn on a few lights as we go, but I've locked the door and kept the closed sign on it, since it's after five and I'm hoping to keep Logan away.

He texted earlier, and I made the excuse that I'd be working late at the Country Club with Rosie, so hopefully he doesn't notice anything amiss. He mentioned having dinner with his parents, so I know he'll be busy for a while and won't see my car.

Sage leans on the kitchen doorframe while I take care of the cats, Tabby meandering in and checking her out as I fill the bowls. An unusual occurrence for her not to race to hers and gobble down the food, but she seems quite entranced with Sage. Cat and witch stare at each other for a long moment, before Sage says, "Once or twice."

"Awesome." That doesn't exactly reassure me, but seeing as

I've *never* done it, I try to stay positive. "I really appreciate this. I'm kind of at my wit's end right now and this is far outside my field of expertise."

Something passes between her and the cat, and Tabitha relinquishes her stare to eat. Arthur and Lancelot have nearly finished and it's probably wise for her to claim her portion or they'll happily devour it, too.

"Would you like something to drink?"

Sage reaches into her big bag and withdraws a travel mug. "I came prepared."

My nerves are shaking so badly, I'm dying to have a glass of wine, but figure it's probably better if I don't. Some of Rosie's leftover cider is still in the crockpot, so I grab a cup and heat it in the microwave as the cats begin cleaning their paws. "I believe I have all the ingredients, but I'm not exactly sure of the steps. And, I never found a preacher who fit the knock-em down variety Paris said I'd need. I'm prepared for whatever type of spell we need, but they all seem a bit...complicated."

She shrugs out of her jacket, a sort of patchwork quilt with mismatched buttons. "It's not that hard. The important thing is doing everything in the right order."

"I did not realize that," I comment, removing the warmed cider and taking a sip. My stomach is empty and I feel it sliding down and pooling in it. "And the preacher?"

"Would be nice for insurance, but we'll manage."

Wish I had her confidence. "There's one thing I'd like to do before we start."

She shrugs. "I'm in no hurry."

I sort of am, since Dad will eventually come home, and Logan will want to see me. I go to Aunt Willa's desk and pull out the paper I've copied the sigils from the box on.

I show Sage the attic, the cats following. She eyes the spot I've prepared on the floor and nods, signaling it will do.

I give her the items from the shop and she opens her bag, removing various tools. She lines all of them up, closes her eyes and says a prayer over them.

Done with that, she goes about drawing a circle with a pentagram inside, adding candles, and pouring black salt around the outer perimeter. She settles, legs crossed, near the bottom of the circle and closes her eyes once more. Her lips move silently.

"I'll be back in a minute," I tell her, picking up the chalk.

She doesn't respond, continuing her inaudible words, and I make my exit.

If a hex box works because of the sigils on the sides, why I can't I use a similar method on my house? Winter suggested it and it seemed like a form of insurance, too. If Cocheta escapes the attic, maybe they'll still bind her to the building.

One way or another, I'm going to get her ghost to cross over, but I'm not taking chances that she'll flee before I manage that.

I start at the east side of the house, following the layout from the box I've copied to the paper. Winter has given me specific phrases to empower them. As I draw the first sigil and say the words, I see it glow slightly in the murky twilight. When I draw the second on the north this one also glows, but brighter.

By the time I make it around to sketch the final sigil, its glow is bright enough to blind me for a moment. Feeling more confident, I return to the attic.

Sage is still seated but cracks an eye open at my approach. "Bring me the necklace."

I do as instructed, keeping it in the hex box. She rises to take it and places it in the center of the pentagram. "It would be more powerful if we had two more witches."

"I can come up with one."

She glances over to the rocking chair in the corner. I follow her gaze and find Tabitha washing her face with her paw. "Yep,"

I confirm. "She's my great-grandmother several times removed, and from what I've been able to ascertain, she falls in that category."

I call to the feline, but of course, she ignores me. Marching over, I reach down and pick her up, ignoring her cries. "Where do you want her?" I ask.

Sage smirks, pointing to the circle. "Place her in the north, since she is your ancestor. You take the south." Her finger moves to the opposite side.

I set Tabitha down at the top of the pentagram and take the spot across from her. Persephone appears and examines the setup. "Do you know what you're doing?" she asks.

Sage looks right at her, and I realize she can hear her, too. Maybe see her.

"I think we have a pretty good handle on things," I tell the angel.

She's wearing outrageous layers of pink and purple eyeshadow, a bright green scarf, and a flowing dress with rhinestones sewn into it. She hovers and leans toward the hex box, screwing up her nose. "I have the feeling this is well beyond what you and this girl can control. I think I better stay."

To be honest, Persephone makes me nervous when she's not annoying me. "A lovely idea," I say, hoping my voice doesn't give away my doubts. I glance at Sage. "Is that okay?"

Sage gives me a one-shoulder shrug. "All the same to me. Are you a witch?" she asks Persephone.

Persephone sniffs. "Spirit guide."

Sage scrutinizes her a moment, then switches to the hex box. "Let's do this."

She closes her eyes and I follow suit, but before we can begin, Sherlock materializes. "You can't do this without me," he announces.

He floats directly across from Persephone, each at a point on the pentagram. I feel a surge of electricity as all of our energies suddenly connect. Sage opens an eye and looks at the ghost, raising a brow to me.

I mimic her and shrug. "It can't hurt, can it?"

I'm sort of relieved she can see and hear the spirits and I don't have to explain.

She shakes out her fingers as if releasing some of the energy flowing through the circle and sighs. "If you're going to help, you have to promise not to interfere with my spell."

"Interfere?" Apparently, she knows the ghost better than I do, and now I'm worried about his presence. "What do you mean by that?" I demand of them.

Persephone *tsks*. "We don't need you," she insists to him. "You better be on your way and let us deal with this."

The two begin arguing, and I rub my forehead. "Enough!" I'm tired of having to intervene in all of these arguments lately, but it seems like I have no choice. "I'll kick both of you out if you can't behave yourselves."

Glaring at them over the circle, I notice Tabby grinning.

Not the type suggesting she's enjoying this, but one that tells me she has a secret.

I'm honestly not sure if I can trust any of them, but I have no choice.

Persephone rolls her eyes at my threat and looks away, crossing her arms. Sherlock simply appears abashed and nods.

"Okay then." I take a deep breath and motion Sage to continue. "Please continue."

Once more, she draws herself up, closing her eyes and reciting a blessing of protection.

Her voice is mesmerizing, reassuring. I try to tune out everything pertaining to my dad's innocence, my parents in general, and the ball, pulling up Logan's face to calm and center me.

Before we get to the first step of the un-hexing, the lights flicker and the candles blow out.

Clear as day, a man's voice booms in the small space. *"Your daddy's gonna pay for what he did to me!"*

Startled, I open my eyes and gasp.

Sean O'Reilly's ghost is bearing down on me.

Chapter Twenty

His hands are like claws, nails elongated, and he swipes at me.

I scream and jump back.

My body is wracked with a frigid chill, but the attack does nothing more. No searing pain, as Sean passes right through me.

Heart thumping, I glare at him as he circles overhead. "My father didn't kill you. Haylee Dean did."

The ghost makes a crazy laughing noise, even though his lips don't move. His eyes are wild and his spectral form trembles, the shape fading in and out, like a TV relying on rabbit ears that can't quite get a strong reception. "*Your daddy will paaayyy.*"

He launches himself at me again, but this time I don't move. His claw goes through my abdomen this time, his energy baptizing me in bitter cold before he soars and loops upward to the rafters.

"Come back and tell me what happened that day," I yell, but he disappears at the peak, the white apparition turning into nothing but wisps that vanish.

Shaking from the overdose of adrenaline, I bounce on the

balls of my feet a few times, shaking out my hands like Sage did earlier.

"Are you okay?" she asks.

"Fine." I steady myself once more. "Sorry about that. I have a lot going on right now, and along with breaking this hex, I'm trying to solve a murder mystery."

She seems undisturbed, almost intrigued. "Cool."

Something like that.

Persephone taps a foot, the shoe making no sound, which kind of dilutes the impatience of the action. "Can we get started now?"

What does she have to be in a hurry about? She's dead! Well, not alive in the corporeal sense, anyway. "After this, you're going to help me track down Sean's killer," I tell her, "and don't give me any backtalk about how you can't tell me anything. Even if you can't, you can give me clues, big ones and fast."

She lifts her chin in defiance like a spoiled child, but I know she'll come through. I've come to realize her act is exactly that. While she pretends she doesn't like her guardian angel role, I think she enjoys it immensely.

As our energies reconnect, Tabby stands on all four feet, looking alert and flicking her tail.

Sherlock adjusts his glasses and rolls his shoulders. "I'd feel better about this if we'd located the preacher."

Persephone hovers in place. "I've put out a call to one who'll show up if needed."

We all stare at her and she gives us a tiny shrug. "What? I'm connected to a lot of various kinds of spirits. I leaned on somebody who can help. If we need him, he'll come."

I'm not sure whether to feel worried or relieved.

Sage nods. "Third times a charm, right?"

Her attempt at humor makes me chuckle, even though my nerves are strung tight. I tell myself to relax and trust Persephone. She talks a lot of smack, but she comes through when my backside is on the line.

Pretty sure it is right now. "I hope this works."

"Ninety-nine percent of a successful spell is intention, Ava." Sage winks. "It will work if you believe it will."

Closing my eyes, I repeat *I believe, I believe, I believe.* I let the echo of her words calm my heartbeat and align my energy with that of the spell as she begins reciting it.

We chant, the energy flows, and when the moment's right, I do as Sage instructs—I call on Cocheta with all my might.

Sage waves a hand at the box and the lid flies open. Inside the necklace lays unmoving, as if asleep.

More chanting, our voices rising.

Tabby's eyes turn a shiny gold color, the supernatural light seeming to almost lift her body off the floor.

Persephone is serious now, her brow furrowed with concentration. Sherlock holds out his hands toward the box, but I can't tell if he's trying to summon the necklace, or ward against it.

"Call her name three times," Sage instructs.

"Cocheta Bonham Reynaud." I repeat it twice more. "I summon you to come forth."

The necklace trembles, the locket flies open.

Deep inside my belly, fear roils. The blood pumping through my heart seems to grow cold. My legs shake, my hands buzzing from the energy and magick. I swallow hard, her name like a rough pit in my throat.

"What's happening?" I whisper when no ghost appears.

Sage chews her gum in consternation, smacking it loudly and blowing a bubble. "Try again."

I raise my voice, firming it. "Cocheta Bonham Reynaud, I command you to come forth."

The necklace rises as if by invisible hands. It turns slowly around the circle, the locket's two halves stopping as though they are eyes looking at me.

"Who calls me forth?" A woman's voice, clear and authoritative, rings out.

Mamma Nightengale warned me not to give my name to Cocheta. Names have great power, and so I'm careful as I answer. "I am the granddaughter of a great and powerful witch, and I'm prepared to break the curse that keeps you bound in that jewelry."

There's a long, pregnant pause. The locket hovers near my face. *"What motive would you have to perform such an act? What is the price?"*

I force as much confidence as I can into my reply. "In return for your freedom, you must do my bidding."

Cocheta laughs, the sound echoing in the room. "I do no witch's bidding."

The locket falls to the floor at my feet, lifeless.

I swallow against the tightness in my throat and glance around. The circle should be holding her spirit, but I can't see it. "Where did she go?" I hiss.

We all scan the area. Shoulder shrugs and shaking heads tell me no one else can see or sense her either.

Sage points to the necklace, which begins vibrating. "She's still trapped."

It takes turns bouncing toward each of us, stopping when it touches the edge of the circle and jumping back. Checking the boundaries.

Then it swivels and dives for the space between me and Persephone. Once more, it hits the chalk and salt and springs backward, like a robot vacuum that keeps bumping into a wall.

Phew. The circle seems to be doing its job. "I have a simple request," I explain as she continues to try and penetrate the circle. "One that's straightforward and benefits us both."

The locket floats in the air, whizzing around the perimeter, continuing to look for weak spots.

I throw out my last offensive move. "If you refuse, Cocheta. I will bind you in there for another two hundred years."

The locket pauses, hovers.

I suck in a breath when it races back to dangle right in front of my face.

I steel myself. Sage told me I cannot break the circle, and I force my feet to stay planted.

As it flutters up and down my body, I sense Cocheta is sniffing me. I almost check my underarms to see if my deodorant has failed.

Finally, she speaks, a haughty sound. *"You have no power."*

Since I'm not sure if I do or don't, I resist engaging in a pissing contest with her. I feel the tick-tock of time running out. "This circle contains a great amount of it, and you know it."

Persephone and Sage stare at me, and I wish I could read their minds. Did I say something wrong?

Then I realize they aren't looking at me. I feel a hand on my shoulder. My chest warms.

"She's trying to intimidate you," my aunt whispers in my ear.

"Aunt Willa?"

Her beautiful face fades in and out next to me. *"The only person who lacks power in this room is her."*

I stare at the locket, feeling more confident. "Seems to me you don't have many options," I tell Cocheta. "You were cursed by a preacher's daughter. Not even a real witch, like yourself. Magick is an equal opportunity employer. You don't own it."

Another ghost appears near Sherlock. He's dressed in a white shirt, black pants, and wears a large gold cross around his neck. "She's right, Cocheta. What my daughter did to you was wrong, and you had every right to be angry about your land and what happened, but it's time for us to put all of these trespasses to rest."

All of us, including Tabby, stare wide-eyed at the preacher.

Everyone, that is, except Persephone. "You got my message."

He offers a cryptic grin. "For you, Seph, anything."

He winks and I nearly fall over.

"You're Birdie's father." *Stop flirting with my guardian angel.*

His grin turns to me. "I'd say *in the flesh,* but we all know that's inaccurate. In the spirit, so it appears."

Another wink.

A new surge of energy ripples through the circle. Tabby shapeshifts.

Into her *naked* female form.

Everyone's attention obviously swings to her. "Tabitha," I warn.

The necklace whirls to face preacher however. *"You!"*

As we watch, Billie Dupree raises a hand in the air, peeling his gaze away from my grandmother. "In the name of our Lord, I release the curse placed upon you, Cocheta Bonham Reynaud. Your sins are washed away, as is the binding that holds you."

Sage and I exchange a worried glance. This isn't part of our spell.

The necklace flies straight up in the air, and then crashes down, exploding in front of our eyes. The hex box erupts in flames.

From them emerges the ghost of Christmas Past—a beautiful dark-skinned woman.

Her hair is braided, an intricately beaded cape on her shoulders. It covers a beautiful, garnet colored dress underneath.

Her dark eyes are vivid and intense, glowing with an energy I don't like. Anger, hatred, revenge.

She flies inside the circle, stretching and growing larger. "I'll take what's mine," she screams at me as she passes. "I denounce your offer."

"What have you done?" I ask Dupree.

He continues holding out his hand, and doesn't seem concerned in the least. "Don't you fret now, Miss Ava. I've got this under control."

He winks a third time, but his forehead is creased. In worry or consternation?

I believe, I believe, I believe.

But I don't. This wasn't how it was supposed to go, and now I'm not sure what to do.

I hold my ground, but then Sage yells, "Look out!"

Tabby screeches, Persephone calls my name, and I hear Aunt Willa in my head say, *"Duck!"*

Cocheta latches onto me.

She breaks right through the salt line, her cold, ghostly fingers grabbing me around the neck. Unlike Sean, she's able to touch me, her non-corporeal fingers digging deep to cut off my air.

I struggle against her grip, but can't get hold of her. A new kind of energy fills my chest, making my heart beat so hard and fast, I feel as if it will explode like the necklace.

As Cocheta's dark eyes bore into mine, I sense black magick flooding through me.

I see Tabitha step toward us. I fall to my knees, but the black magick doesn't let go. Cocheta's gaze fills my vision and the room fades away.

I hear the preacher shout for divine intervention right before everything goes dark.

Chapter Twenty-One

I wake to a heavy gray mist and hear the murmur of voices around me. Some are close, others far away.

A heaviness presses in on my ears.

My skin prickles at the sensation of ghosts. The mist is thick, and I have the sense to stay quiet and not alert the spirits that I'm among them.

Glancing down, I realize my body is fading in and out of itself, my astral half disengaging from the flesh and bone that keeps me human. My head hurts, and below my throat, where Cocheta's fingers were wrapped, I feel slightly numb.

I need to get back, I think, but the idea is slippery and as misty as the fog.

The attic. Right? I need to return there to…

What? I can't remember.

What I do remember is this feeling. I can't feel my pulse anymore, don't seem to have a heartbeat. I can't help the whimpering that comes from my throat. Have I died again?

Oh no. My brain clears slightly. *Not here. Not now.*

I have to get back to the attic.

Where I am now is a little too close to the other side.

The last time my near-death experience was over in a flash, and I only saw Aunt Willa, but this time?

If I were to guess, this is some in-between dimension—not the physical 3D world, and not the afterlife either. Like a waiting room, before you move on.

The murmurings of the other ghosts fall silent. Predators listening for their prey.

Cocheta is here. Sean might be as well.

Keeping my own silence, I mentally send out an SOS. *Aunt Willa? Can you help me?*

It's not my aunt who appears, but Sherlock. "We need to get you out of here."

No kidding. I sense that he's been in the in-between many times, and that's how he hangs around in the underground library with Paris and London. I reach out as if to take his hand, then remember both of us are not corporeal. I'm worried to speak out loud, but he did, so... "What do we do?"

"Follow me," he says.

I watch him walk away, and I start to follow, hoping I go unnoticed, but then the mist absorbs him. I try to catch up, but can't see where he went.

Panic rising, I begin running.

The next thing I know, the fog clears, and I'm standing in a yard, looking at a farmhouse. There's a wagon wheel half buried in the ground out front, an old well and pumping station nearby. There's something familiar about the residence, and I scan the landscape—it too resembles another that I know.

In the distance is a hill, and my memory superimposes a picture of how it looks now, with long rows of grapevines. The scene I'm looking at is devoid of those, and a giant oak tree stands sentry on the hill.

There's a woman at the well, pumping water into a bucket. Three children—two boys and a girl—play tag in the yard.

They're barefoot with dirty faces. As she heaves the bucket

and begins to haul her load to the house, I notice the long skirt of her dress, the bun on her head.

In my mind, I fill in the scene the way I know it. The house is three times bigger, thanks to flamboyant improvements and expansion. To the left a hundred yards away is a building that might be a speakeasy in the future

The Cross family homestead.

Another young boy comes out of a horse barn. He's in his teens and his features remind me of Logan. A third, this one older, joins him, two fishing poles in hand. They pass several horses in a pasture, heading for a path snaking through the woods. "Be back by dinner," their mother shouts.

They wave acknowledgment and disappear.

"Excuse me." I follow her toward the house.

She glances over her shoulder, water sloshing over the lip of the bucket as she halts mid-step. Her face morphs into fear and she waves a hand at the children playing. "Get in the house!"

They ignore her and continue their game.

"I mean you no harm," I say. "You wouldn't happen to be Birdie May, would you?"

Logan told me his great-grandfather and -grandmother bought this acreage at the turn of the twentieth century, but I'm wondering if it was actually part of his mother's family long before that.

The woman shouts at her youngest children once more, getting their attention from the no-nonsense tone of her voice.

As they run for the house, she pins me with a fierce look. "Get thee from me, Satan."

I've been called a lot of things, but the devil isn't one of them. "I need your help. I swear I'm not going to harm you or your children."

The kids rush past, ignoring me, and I realize they can't see me. She can, but wants nothing to do with me.

She shoves them inside and goes to enter herself. I lunge forward to grab her, but my hand goes through her arm.

Right. I'm a ghost.

She slams the screen and then the inner door, and I stand there thinking that if she's not Birdie, she can't help me, but there must be a reason I'm here in this sliver of time and space.

I scan the landscape. There are woods everywhere, and I see all the work that has gone into the land, the house, the fences, the barn. Was this Cocheta's at one point? Has Birdie already cursed her into the necklace?

I have to find out.

I test my ability to move through solid objects by sticking my hand through the door. I don't feel anything other than air, so I stick my head through, too.

I'm looking into a kitchen. The woman is dipping cups into the bucket of water and giving one to each of the kids. She tells them they must go upstairs to play now, and they whine and complain. When she turns to set their dishes in the sink, a sharp rebuke on her tongue, she jumps at the sight of my head, peering into her house.

Commanding them to run as fast as they can, she yanks a cross necklace out from under the collar of her dress. "You cannot come into this house, demon! I will not let you harm my family."

The children go screaming from the room. I step fully through, and she stumbles back, running into a wooden table. "What year is it?" I ask.

She holds up the cross, so similar to her father's, and marches toward me. "Get thee from me," she yells, and shoves her empty hand at my face as if she will blast me with righteous power.

"Sorry, but that won't work. I'm not a demon," I repeat. "I'm just a person like you, and I happen to be in the wrong time and space. But I think there's a reason for that."

She doesn't know what to do now, and removes the jewelry from around her neck, holding it out as if she will back me up through the door and from her house. I reach out and act as though I will touch the cross, and my fingers go right through it. "See?"

"A spirit!" She lowers the cross, fear in her eyes. "Please don't hurt my children."

"I have no intention of hurting anyone. I simply want to ask for your help. My request is for your progeny—a great-great-grandson. He's very important to me. I think I...I love him, and well..." I'm blubbering and smiling now at the thought of Logan. "He's quite a guy, and he probably got some of his awesomeness from you."

Her eyes narrow and I realize she may not know the term 'awesome.' "Is he a spirit, too?"

"Not yet, but he could be if I don't work some magick here, and not that stage trick stuff. Have you cursed a witch into a necklace recently?"

Her face blanches and she jerks back again. "Magick is evil. I'll not have any in my home."

There's a tingling that starts in my extremities, my fingers and toes growing cold. I glance at my hand, and see my digits beginning to disappear. I don't know what that is, but it can't be good. "Look, I don't have much time. If you are Birdie May, and you haven't cursed Cocheta Reynaud into a necklace yet, I need you to please do me a favor. Try to work things out with her. I know she's demanding something you can't give, but there has to be common ground."

At that moment, Persephone pops in, startling us both. "Tread carefully, Ava. You shouldn't try to change history."

History is going to have to take a backseat. "There has to be a way for you and Cocheta to work things out," I insist to Birdie. "If you don't, your great-great grandson in the future is going to pay the price."

"Or not even be born if you set the wrong things in motion," the angel chimes.

She glances between Persephone and me. "I don't understand who you are or how you got here, but you must leave."

To Persephone, I ask, "She is Birdie, right?"

The angel acknowledges it's true. "She's working some magick that neither one of us wants to get tangled up in." ,

"I am not!" Birdie insists.

I ignore her. "I'm already tangled up in it, if you haven't noticed, Seph. And what's up with you and the preacher?"

Persephone appears to blush. Who knew a spirit guide could feel embarrassed? "Nothing we need to discuss right now."

"Fine." I turn to Birdie. "I'm not kidding when I say this is serious. You're messing around with curses and it's dangerous stuff. This isn't a little powder to make people pass out. It's going to come back to haunt your descendants. Whatever you do, do not try to outsmart Cocheta. Make amends, smooth things over, somehow, some way. Give her back a piece of this land for her family. She's a mother like you, and this small thing can change the future for your offspring for the better, and whatever magick you do have—"

She waves the cross and shakes her head. "I don't believe in it. I will *not* have it in my house."

My legs are beginning to disappear, my arms as well. "Drop the act. I know you're dabbling in spells you shouldn't be, and I know you believe you're protecting your family. Your dad was a stage magician, but you hold real power. You must use it wisely, Birdie. This sort of dark magick isn't something to play with."

She puts the necklace back on. "Get out of my house. I am a God-fearing woman and I will not stand for this sort of thing."

If I weren't rapidly fading away, I'd stay and prove her wrong. "His name is Logan. Logan Cross. Please think of him when you're deciding what to do with Cocheta."

It's the last I can get out before my chest disappears and then I'm floating.

I hear voices calling me. One in particular causes a warm sensation to bloom in my chest.

As if I am Dorothy spinning in a cyclone, I feel my body becoming real again, piece by piece. There's compression on my chest, warm breath inflating my lungs. Suddenly, I'm lying on the floor in the attic, looking up into a face I know and love.

"She's awake," Logan says with a whoosh of breath.

A warm, sloppy dog tongue licks my cheek.

Logan runs a hand over his face. "You have to quit doing this." My quizzical look spurs him to continue. "Dying on me."

I chuckle. "What are you doing here?" *And please tell me Tabby is back to her cat form.*

Sage comes into view, standing behind him and peering down at me. "It appears he has a strong connection to you, could be a past life or something. Good thing he showed up. He brought you out of the in-between when I couldn't."

Drool from Moxley lands on my arm. Tabitha strolls into my line of sight, her cat lips curving with amusement.

Smiling at Logan's serious face, I realize that he's brought me back to life for a second time.

Chapter Twenty-Two

I have a lot of explaining to do over the next two days.

Cocheta disappeared and hasn't been seen or heard from since. Not sure if the sigils didn't work, or she's hiding inside the house somewhere.

Holding out hope, I pray for the best-case scenario—she's moved onto the afterlife.

Logan is understandably confused about what Sage and I were doing in the attic, and I decide not to tell him the truth until I'm sure there's no fallout from releasing the ghost. Instead, I mention crossing over a stubborn spirit who went crazy on me, and he accepted it, but I see the skepticism in his eyes at times when he looks at me.

Sage told me to call her if I have future issues with hexes or ghosts. Logan appears to be safe, and I've made him wear the necklace Raven gave me, against his arguments, just in case.

In exchange, he made me see Doc to assure everyone my "vapors," as Mama deemed it, was not a symptom of some underlying health issue.

Doc gave me the all clear. Persephone and Sherlock have been AWOL. Daddy and Mama have been watching me closely, and I guess it's worth it, since they're forced to hang out with each other in order to do so.

The ball is an hour away, and Mama and I are waiting at my place for Logan to pick us up. While she originally planned to go with Sean, now as luck would have it, she's going with Dad.

I couldn't be happier. Well, maybe a little. Detective Jones still hasn't caught Sean's killer, and I almost wish the ghost would come back so I could get the truth out of him. Not that I could take that to Detective Jones, but there's a murderer running loose, and Dad remains a suspect.

He's meeting us at the Country Club. Rosie has him checking the sound system for the ball.

"I should go with the green dress," Mama says, brushing her hand across her belly as she stares at herself in Aunt Willa's full-length mirror upstairs. "I better run home and change."

We've decked her out in a hot red number, complete with ruby drop earrings and matching bracelet. She's stunning and will knock Dad's socks off. "Don't be silly. This is your color."

She eyes herself, turning one way, then the other. "I do like this outfit."

"Dad loves you in red."

She shakes a finger at me. "Don't be getting your hopes up about us reconciling."

Too late. "Of course not," I say with an insincere face. "But I appreciate the two of you getting along and putting aside your differences. It's been a long time since we've spent Christmas together. It means a lot to me."

Logan arrives a few minutes later, and I drool when he gets out of his Porsche and comes to the door. He's dressed in a formal tux and I suddenly have visions of walking down the aisle, him waiting for me at the end under a twinkling, light-filled arch.

I remove the faux white mink wrap from the window mannequin as Mama lets him in.

He smiles, telling her how beautiful she is, making her blush. Then he finds me in the display.

His eyes shine as he scans me from head to toe. "I'm not sure how I'm going to keep my hands off you for the next few hours."

Mama clears her throat. "I'll be in the car."

I giggle as she escapes and heat rises in my cheeks. That's what Logan does to me—makes me feel carefree and loved.

He also has a knack for saving my life.

I showcase the gown I'm wearing, turning in a circle. "You like it?"

Brax's friend did a bang-up job with my sketch. She took an off-the-rack ivory sheath and layered rows of chiffon and beads from top to bottom. It's not exactly my design, but it's beautiful and I feel quite pretty in it.

"You look amazing." He helps me down from the display and touches my wavy 1920s do, and the poinsettia pinned above my left ear. "I feel like we should be going to the speakeasy for bootleg, rather than the ball."

At least for tonight, maybe he'll let me off the hook about what was going on upstairs. "I'm looking forward to having one-on-one time with you tonight."

He kisses me long and deep and I pray the red lipstick Brax carefully layered on me doesn't rub off.

The dress shimmers under the streetlight as Logan escorts me to the car. I slide into the passenger seat, and I'm glad there are no ghosts hanging around for the moment.

At the Country Club, greenery and white lights outline the ballroom's windows and the entire space sparkles like a winter wonderland. Even the chandeliers have bunches of mistletoe, eucalyptus, and fir, tied with red ribbons.

Dad and the DJ converse on the raised stage and Daddy waves to us when we enter. He jumps down to meet Mama, ogling her before they head to the buffet.

At the other end of the room, Rosie has set up a photo booth with a beautiful Christmas tree backdrop. Couples have their pictures taken before hitting the dance floor.

The food is amazing, and Logan and I dance to nearly every song. His hand feels good on my lower back, and I'm glad I'm not a ghost tonight. To physically feel, smell, hear, and enjoy this lovely evening, is a gift in itself.

"This may be the best holiday ever," I say during a slow dance, my head on his shoulder.

"Is that so?"

He gently whirls me around and around until we are in a shadowed corner. From his pocket he withdraws a clump of mistletoe. "Some of this looks strangely like what my mom had at her house."

"We had trouble with our supply, and she was generous enough to donate hers."

Montgomery and Helen Cross arrive, arm in arm. Over Logan's shoulder, I watch her scan the room.

Looking for me.

I wanted to tell her Logan was safe sooner, but I needed to be sure. Since nothing has happened since the showdown in the attic, I'm feeling more confident.

Logan raises the mistletoe over our heads and we kiss.

Speaking to Helen drops to the bottom of my list of things I have to do.

My eyes are closed, so I don't notice when the lights go out. It's the audible gasps of the crowd and the fact the music dies that brings me out of the stupor Logan's skillful lips have created.

He breaks the kiss just as the emergency lighting comes on over the exits, throwing a red glow over the crowd.

"What's going on?" I ask, squinting through the shadows.

"Must have blown a fuse or something," he replies.

That makes sense.

So why do I have a sinking feeling in my stomach?

Walking toward the dance floor once more, the moonlight from the windows slanting bars across it, I search for Rosie and see her hustling toward the door. "Everyone stay put," she calls out. "I'll get this fixed in a minute."

She exits, and some people follow, probably to head to the restrooms. I figure I'd better get up on stage and try to keep the crowd calm.

The DJ hands me the mic and I'm about to make an announcement, when I notice a faint shimmering energy floating through the crowd.

I blink, trying to clear my sight, and squint again. *Maybe it's a trick of the moonlight.*

The energy morphs into a shape.

Not moonlight.

A face appears, the spectral becoming more solid.

I know that face. It haunted my dreams last night. "Oh no."

Cocheta finds her quarry, stopping behind Helen.

"Look out!" I cry, throwing up an arm as if I can save her.

The ghost grabs Helen around the neck.

Chapter Twenty-Three

Helen claws at her throat, but her hands can't grab Cocheta's. While the ghost has some sort of ability to make contact like a corporeal person, she's still nonphysical and ethereal.

My own neck sears with pain—a phantom memory.

Helen falls to her knees, and people cry out. Montgomery reaches for her but Cocheta yanks her away from him.

I jump from the stage, twisting my ankle when one high-heeled shoe goes sideways. I barely register the pain as I run to the two women locked in a struggle. "Leave her alone!"

Logan runs to his mother as well, and we reach her at the same time. She's now prone on the floor, Cocheta on top. Helen makes choking noises, her eyes rolling up in her head.

Logan grabs his mother's shoulders. It looks like she's choking and I know my hero is about to attempt to help. Cocheta swears and I swat at her, but my hand passes through, connecting with Logan instead.

He gives me a look as I nearly knock him to the floor.

"Sorry!"

My mother's voice rings out loud and clear. "Everyone move back."

She's taking charge like she is so good at doing. The folks gathered are like deer in the headlights, trying to figure out what's happening. They yell questions. "Is she choking? Is she having a heart attack?"

"Get off of her," I command the ghost.

Logan gives me another funny look.

"I'm trying to help her," he says.

"Not you." I lower my voice. "There's a ghost strangling her."

I hear several guests close by suck in a breath in unison, and I'm pretty sure one of them is my mother. Once again, I hear her say, "Give them some air, please. Move back."

Dad gets in on it as well, coaxing the crowd away.

Logan's face contorts. "A ghost?" Thankfully he knows about my abilities. "What do we do?"

I honestly don't know. I look into Helen's fearful face. "Tell her your sorry."

Of course, she can't do anything but struggle for her life. I snap my fingers at Cocheta drawing her attention. "Give her some air and let her speak."

Cocheta jeers at me. "I will have my revenge on every one of Birdie's descendants." She shoots a glance at Logan. "I'm saving you for last."

Persephone and Sherlock appear behind Logan, all smiles. Persephone is laughing as if he just shared a joke.

"Help Helen!" I yell at her.

They both snap to attention, hovering on either side of the melee. Everyone else is witnessing me speaking to ghosts and spirit guides, but to them it appears I'm talking to thin air.

Logan grits his teeth. He's freaking out. "Quit worrying about them and help my mother."

"I'm trying to," I assure him.

"I know what Birdie and her family did to you," I say to

Cocheta. "None of it was fair or right, but revenge solves nothing. It doesn't change the past, and it doesn't make you feel better in the long run. You're not even human anymore. You're a spirit, and you need to cross over and move on."

She releases Helen, who coughs and spits.

As I stare into her eyes, I wonder, does she not realize she's dead?

That can't be.

She stares at her hands a moment, as if seeing them for the first time.

"You're dead, Cocheta," I say softly. "It's time for you to move on."

The sound starts so low, I don't notice it until I realize her body is trembling slightly. Then the sound of her laughter builds, shooting frosty shivers down my spine.

Without warning, she reaches out and grabs hold of me.

I don't know how she has so much strength for a ghost, but she manages to shove a hand through my chest and grip my heart. "I want revenge."

The sensation of her inside my chest makes me want to scream. My extremities lock up and I can't breathe.

"What will that solve?" I gasp out. "Your anger is directed at Birdie, not Helen. Birdie was a witch who cursed you into that necklace then burned your dolls."

Logan is helping his mother sit up. Someone brings her water. The onlookers have fallen silent, listening, and I hear Mrs. Cross try to save face, her voice raw. "That's not true," she says, her voice raw. "She's had a little too much to drink, I think."

Everyone is staring at me, including my mother, with a look of horror on their faces. I'm not sure if they realize I'm talking to a ghost, or think I've gone mad.

My heart feels like it's going to burst.

"No one messes with my family and gets away with it," Cocheta hisses in my face.

Every breath burns like fire. "I love my family, too," I choke out. "I'd do anything for them. But I can't let you hurt the man I love. You were wronged, and I'm sorry for that, but you might think twice about crossing me and causing even more problems for yourself."

"Hurt me?" Logan echoes.

She snickers. "You can't harm me."

"Not true," Persephone argues.

In the past few months, she and Winter have been training me in ways to get earthbound spirits to cross over and stop hanging around the physical plane. It doesn't always work, but in my mind's eye I focus on creating a bright white light a few feet away.

Persephone gives me a thumbs-up and steps to one side of it. Sherlock follows her cue and steps to the other. I have no idea how to trick this ghost into crossing over, but I better think of something fast.

"I spoke to Birdie," I tell her. "The last time you tried to kill me. Went back in time...told her what was about to happen. She's sorry for what she did to you and promised to make amends, change the bad history between you. In another time-line, the two of you are friends."

"Liar," she snarls, but her grip eases a smidge.

"If you move on to the afterlife, you can find her and talk about it. She'll confirm what I'm telling you. You worked it out, forgave each other."

The hatred in her face abates, surprising me. The strain around her eyes and mouth softens. "I don't believe you."

Now who's lying? I can breathe again. She wants to believe it, even if she's skeptical. "Ask Persephone. She was there when I spoke to Birdie and changed your history."

Cocheta glances at the angel, who gives her a smile. "Birdie's on the other side of that light." She points, getting in on the game. "Waiting for you. She wants to tell you how sorry she is. Your kids are there, too. They're excited that you're finally coming home."

Her grip on my heart lessens another degree. I hear people murmuring, asking Logan and Mama if I'm okay or having a fit.

As if we've called her, a familiar figure steps through the light. "Cocheta, it's time to come with me."

Birdie.

No one can see her except me and the other spirits, but as I look at her, the crowd follows my gaze. Birdie glances at me, and then her father joins her, coming to stand by her right side.

He puts a hand on her shoulder, his voice booming out. "We did you wrong, Cocheta." I wonder if he knows no one can hear him. "We want to make it up to you."

Like a balloon losing its air, Cocheta deflates. Tears well in her eyes and her voice shakes as she speaks to Birdie. "We're friends now? How?"

Birdie hesitates. Her father squeezes her arm.

She nods, and I see Cocheta trying to wrap her mind around the idea that something in the past has changed. "Come with us and leave these poor folks alone."

Cocheta takes a step toward them. "My boys are there in the light?"

Birdie gazes at Helen, then Logan. She gives each of her progeny a smile, even though they can't see her. "Everyone you loved is there. A lot has happened in the time you've been in the necklace, and I'm real sorry about that. We have a lot to tell you."

The crowd begins murmuring, not able to hear the conversation. I back away from Cocheta and Logan grabs my arm, pulling me to his side. Helen glares at me, and I give her a reassuring smile. "They're working things out."

Both she and Logan glance toward the space where the light is. "The ghosts?" Logan asks.

"Shh." His mother smacks his hand, eagle eyes scanning the crowd. She raises her scratchy voice. "I'm fine. I got a piece of shrimp caught in my throat from the appetizers, that's all."

Logan and I exchange a knowing smile. "I just need another minute," I tell him.

"Let's freshen up drinks," he calls to the group and most saunter toward the bar. Montgomery drags Helen in that direction, too. "What is going on?" I hear him murmur to her.

Cocheta stares at me over her shoulder. "If you're lying to me, I'll be back."

I rub the spot over my heart. "I think you'll find things there worth staying for."

The preacher and his daughter reach out their hands, and reluctantly, she accepts their invitation. The two women walk into the light, and Dupree glances back at me. "You did a good thing here."

With another wink, he's gone.

Persephone waves a hand over the light and it disappears. Sherlock heaves a sigh, removing his glasses and going about cleaning them.

I'm so relieved, I slump to the floor.

Mama and Daddy hoist me up. "Are you all right?" Mama asks.

"Yes, but I could use a stiff drink."

Daddy pats my hand. "I'm on it."

Helen returns, Logan beside her. "Well?"

"All done," I tell her.

"You're sure?"

Her son glances back and forth between us. "What just happened?"

"I am," I inform Helen. I lean on Logan's arm. "I'll tell you about it later."

The lights come back on. Everyone cheers.

I snap my fingers at the DJ and the music starts again.

Daddy returns with a cup of spiked punch. He gives a second to Mama. We both gulp it down.

"I think I'll take my folks home," Logan tells me.

"Good idea."

"I'll catch up with you later."

He kisses my forehead and walks away.

As he crosses the floor, Mama and Daddy and I move out of the way of a couple wanting to dance. We stop near the side of the stage, the giant speakers blasting the pop version of Little Drummer Boy.

Rosie returns and waves at me from across the room. I wave back.

I'm debating whether to get another helping of punch or call it a night, when, from out of nowhere, a piece of mistletoe flies across the expanse and smacks me in the face.

"What the...?" I shift in the direction it came from.

My stomach sinks to my feet. "Oh no."

"Miss me?" A flying spectral calls over the noise.

Sean O'Reilly's ghost is back.

Chapter Twenty-Four

He swoops down, but it's not me he's gunning for.

He goes after my parents.

I jump in front of them throwing out my hands. The punch cup crashes to the floor.

His claws swipe through me, and while they do no physical harm, the sharp spikes feel like icicles.

I slam into Mama.

She and Daddy stumble into a tangle of cords and the big, black floor speaker. As they fall in unison with me, Mama's foot catches in a cord and yanks the DJ table over.

Sean rails about my father, and attacks again.

His anger is palpable, and although his ghostly form can do no damage, his electrical energy makes the lights flicker.

The DJ is scrambling to pick up his table, the sound system balking and sending out ear-deafening screeches.

People gasp and stare once more, their expressions signifying they think we've all lost our marbles.

Logan and Helen rush to us. He helps me stand.

Mrs. Cross is still rubbing her neck, but she knows I'm seeing something otherworldly, and the fear in her eyes tells me she assumes it's Cocheta's ghost. "Do something!" she yells at me.

Daddy tries to help Mama untangle her foot. I attempt to calm Sean. "You can't hurt us, so knock it off."

His ghost blows past me so quickly, I feel the ends of my hair lift. One of the chandeliers above our heads trembles.

I fear that he, like Cocheta, may be able to do more damage than most.

An explosion of pops and crackles erupts from the DJ's cords.

"Get Mama out of those," I command Dad.

He looks flustered, trying to figure out what's going on and do what I say at the same time. Logan launches himself in to help.

They want to protect us, but don't understand from what.

Sean aims for me again. His energy acts like a magnet, drawing things to him now. Glass balls from the table decorations, mistletoe from the garlands—all of it coming at me like missiles.

I throw my hands over my head and duck as items pelt me and the stage. Mama cries my name, and in the next moment, anger flares in my stomach. Striding forward, I raise my hands and yell, "Knock it off!"

A strange silence falls and energy ripples up my spine. For a moment, I feel like Billie Dupree, giving the crowd quite a show.

Sean barrels through the large ballroom, creating more havoc. I call for Persephone or Sherlock.

Neither appears.

Frustrated, I stomp my foot. "Persephone, you're lousy at being a guardian angel! I'm putting in a request for a new one."

My outburst echoes through the space. I feel a hand on my shoulder and turn to find Logan.

"What can I do?"

I wish I knew. I squeeze his hand as I say to my father, "It's Sean. Try talking to him, get him to stop."

Mama and Dad ask in unison, "Sean?"

"Tell me you didn't kill him," I say to Daddy under my breath.

"Of course, I didn't." He oozes disgust at the idea.

"Why is he coming after you then?"

Dad looks flustered. "I have no idea other than I told him I was going to win your mother back."

Mama stops scanning for Sean. "You did?"

He takes her hand and draws her to him. "You bet I did. The biggest reason I came home was to see you and persuade you to marry me again."

Another piece of mistletoe lands in my hair. I whirl on Sean. "Stop acting like a spoiled brat," I yell at him. "Whatever your problem is, it doesn't matter now. You're dead! Go to the light, already. Things are great on the other side, you'll love it."

Those still around gawk. Helen rubs a hand over her face. I notice a gal has her phone out recording me.

This will be spread all over Thornhollow before morning.

Persephone still doesn't make an appearance, but suddenly Sherlock is there. "Would you like me to try, dear?"

"Be my guest."

As Sean picks up speed to dive at us once more, Sherlock lifts into the air and intercepts him. He grabs Sean by the lapels and the two begin to tumble and wrestle above our heads.

A spirit fight. *Now I've seen it all.*

I take a step in retreat and run into Logan. His arms go around me. "What's happening?"

"A ghost hitchhiker I picked up the other day is fighting with Sean's ghost."

"Oh, okay," he says, deadpan. "I figured it was something like that."

I jab his ribs with an elbow. "Well, at least this ghost is trying. Persephone has abandoned me."

"Don't give up on her yet." Logan has a soft spot for the angel since she recruited him when I was being held at gunpoint by my former neighbor back in October. "She did help us out last time you had…an issue."

The door flies open and Detective Jones strides in. He pulls up short, observes the messy decorations and disastrous pile of equipment behind us, and frowns.

His gaze lands on Dad. "Nash," he calls as he marches toward us, oblivious to the two ghosts fighting overhead. "Got some news for you."

Sherlock gets the upper hand. Then Sean sucker punches him in the face. I hear his glasses break, and Sherlock lets out a curse.

"Detective," my father says as Jones shoots me a look.

"Sorry to bust in on your party, but I thought you'd want to know. Just got word about the autopsy. O'Reilly didn't die from choking on your guitar pick."

Overhead, Sean stops brawling with Sherlock, pushing him off and glaring at Jones.

"What did he die of?" I ask.

"An overdose." Jones has his hat in his hands and fiddles with the brim. "Your buddy had cancer, Nash. Doc got hold of his medical records and seems he had about six weeks to live. Appears he decided to…"

"No!" Sean screams and dives at us.

Sherlock intercepts him, knocking him aside as Jones finishes. "…take his own life. OD'd on one of his medications right before he went to The Wedding Chapel. He must have stuck the guitar pick in his mouth once he got on the grounds, attempting to make it look like you were responsible."

No wonder he looked so bad! It wasn't alcohol, it was the disease.

And Haylee Dean is innocent.

The news has a ripple effect. My dad's shoulders slump. Mama throws her arms around his neck and hugs him. At the same time, Logan squeezes my shoulder.

"I told you Daddy wasn't a murderer," I tell Jones. "You owe him an apology."

He huffs. "I was going off the evidence."

"Whatever." I turn away from him to hug Dad.

Jones walks away, calling over his shoulder, "Merry Christmas, y'all."

When I release Daddy, I look up to find Sherlock removing his broken glasses. He gives me a salute, then takes Sean by the back of the jacket and shuffles him toward a glowing light on the other side of the room. Travis' ghost is waiting for Sean.

I watch them go into the light together, half wondering if Sherlock is crossing over as well. I feel a little sad at the thought.

Logan touches my cheek. "You're bleeding. We need to get you cleaned up."

"Sorry about the show," I call as Logan leads me out. "Everything's fine now. Let's finish the Mistletoe Ball, shall we?"

Dad jumps on the stage, wrestling the mic from the DJ and waving people forward. "Get everybody back in here," he commands. "We've got good music to dance to and delicious food to eat!"

Rosie runs around, trying to pick up the various table decorations. Several women join in to help. "You okay?" she asks before we're out the door.

"Yes," I tell her and I mean it.

Logan escorts me to the women's restroom. There he dabs a wet towel at my cheek. My hair is a disaster, and somehow my dress is torn.

The cut is minimal, however, and stops bleeding almost immediately. I stare at it in the mirror, and try to fix my hair.

"You look beautiful," he says.

"You're too kind."

"We're going to have lots of time around the fireplace now, and you'll tell me everything, right? The truth this time?"

I sigh. "Do I have a choice?"

"Nope."

"Some of it's not mine to share. You have to ask your mother."

He gives me a doubtful look. "Why do I have the feeling she's not going to open up too easily?"

"Because she won't, but you deserve to hear it from her."

He loosens his tie and tugs the necklace out from under his collar. "Does it have to do with this?"

I nod.

He slips it off and places it on me. "Might be more fun to make you tell me. A bet a tickle session would work."

I hate that and he knows it. "I'm a weakling. I'll cave and tell you everything."

A grin. "Thought so."

We run into his folks on the way back to the event. They're leaving for home.

Helen pulls me aside and lowers her voice. "You're sure it's safe now?"

My very bones are exhausted at this point, but my heart is lighter than it's been since she laid this on me at Halloween.

"Yes," I tell her. "Everyone is."

In an unexpected display of emotion, she wraps her arms around me. Over her shoulder, Logan gives me a surprised expression. It no doubt matches mine.

Helen disengages, slides her hands down her dress to straighten it, and clears her throat. "You two enjoy the rest of your night."

She and his dad leave, and the two of us return to the ball-room. Several guests ask me what happened and I tell them it was just an unexplainable situation with the lights, a crazy gust or two of wind, and some mischievous spirits.

I say the last part with a wink and they chuckle. People don't really want to believe in ghosts, even though they know my aunt claimed to be a medium, and some have discovered I am, too.

Most of the decorations are back in order and Daddy has found a guitar. He stands on stage playing Rock Around the Christmas Tree and couples dance.

Logan and I join in, but soon, he pulls me into a dark corner and holds a piece of mistletoe overhead.

"What do you think you're doing with that?" I tease.

He grins, lowers his head, and kisses me. "Merry Christmas, Ava."

Chapter Twenty-Five

✣✣✣

Christmas dawns bright and cold, cold at least by Georgia standards.

Daddy went home with Mama, so I had the house to myself. Logan and I spent time in our favorite spot on the couch and I fessed up to everything. Forget Helen, I thought. She should've told him what was going on, and it wasn't exactly fair of her to put the burden of secrecy on me.

Logan quietly listened to all of it—from me needing to borrow rent money to fearing I wouldn't be able to stop Cocheta from doing something nasty to him.

As I divulged all, the cats made themselves at home, climbing onto the sofa with us. The illumination from the flames and the twinkling lights on the tree lent a romantic glow. When I was done, Logan stayed silent for another long minute.

"You saved my life," he finally said, staring at the fire.

"You've saved mine twice, so..." I waggled my hands, mimicking a scale. "I still owe you one."

"Life with you is never dull."

The sarcasm in his tone was not appreciated. "Hey, I can't help that I'm cursed with Aunt Willa's gift."

The rest of the evening dissolved into kissing, and eventually, even the felines left us alone.

Come daybreak, I open my eyes to find Tabby toying with the gift Logan gave me before he left at midnight.

The sun coming through my window bounces off the diamonds in the tennis bracelet, causing it to sparkle brighter than anything I've ever seen. Beside it is something worth even more.

The deed to the house. As of today, it's mine.

Retrieving the bracelet from my great-grandmother's claws, I put it on and wonder what I can give him in return that's even a fraction as valuable.

In the kitchen, I discover Rhys has been by, leaving various breads and muffins with a note inviting me over for a celebratory drink at seven.

He and Brax have also left a mint condition, collector's miniature red Porsche on the table. *"Santa thought you might be a bit busy saving your boyfriend and all from an evil witch, as well as playing matchmaker to your parents, to get your Christmas shopping done. Hope this helps."*

Logan will love it. My friends are always taking care of me.

I drink coffee to clear the cobwebs, and feed the cats.

Mama is expecting me for brunch and gift opening in a little while. As I get ready, I talk to my aunt, hoping she can hear me. "It's the first Christmas you won't be here, and I'd sure give anything if you were, but I'm glad you made me come home. Things are good. Really good."

Several friends text me, including Winter, to wish me Merry Christmas. Brax lets me know the video going around town of me at the ball is being "contained."

Whatever that means.

I'm grateful for his technical expertise, and I'm sure I don't want to know anything about his hacking skills.

Logan and I plan to have our own private celebration later this evening, and I have a special bottle from the winery waiting for us. I'm setting it out, with some glasses, when Sean's spirit appears.

I jump, nearly breaking both. "What are you doing here?"

He doesn't attack, his energy calm and his spectral self looking years younger. "Sorry to startle you. I just wanted to say...thank you. And could you give Haylee a message for me?"

Taking a deep breath to slow my pulse, I nod. "Sure. Why not? It's only Christmas after all. Not like I have anything else to do."

Ignoring my sarcasm, he hovers and clears his throat. "I owe her an apology."

"Not only her," I chastise. "Mama and Daddy too."

Again, he ignores me. "Tell her I never meant to hurt her. She's a good person. She should go back to Nashville, follow her dream."

"Are you going to be looking out for her now?"

He confirms my suspicions. "My first assignment as a guardian angel."

"Good luck to you," I say in all sincerity.

He disappears and a bit later, I'm about to go out the door when Persephone materializes. "Where you off to?"

I grab my jacket from the hook. "It's Christmas, in case you haven't noticed. I'm going to spend it with my parents—both of them, together, in the same house. Now *that's* a gift."

"Huh, okay."

She seems miffed I don't invite her along.

"This hasn't happened in years and I'm going to enjoy it."

"As well you should."

I haven't known her long, but I can tell by the way she's

blocking my exit, arms crossed, foot tapping, she's expecting something.

I sigh and give in. "Thank you for your help with Cocheta. Then, like usual, you disappeared and weren't around for the second wave of ghostly attacks."

She ignores my barb. "Have you seen that Sherlock character?"

"I doubt he'll be back. He took Sean's ghost into the light. Crossed him over and went with him."

She plays with a ring on her finger. "I was just starting to like that guy."

I grab my purse. I have a bag stuffed with gifts for my parents and some of Rhys's baked goods. "You have a funny way of showing it when you like someone. You might want to work on your people skills."

Making a noise in her throat, she strides for the living room and plops on the sofa. "You're about to get some good news."

My phone rings, and I set down the presents. The ID on the screen makes my pulse skip.

"Good morning and Joyeaux Noel, *cherie*," Gloria Stone's voice is cheery with her faint French accent. "I wanted to give you an update prior to this, but I didn't want to get your hopes up in case something fell through. We're going to have the complete line of wedding dresses ready by the end of next week!"

"What? You're kidding!"

"You should be able to start taking orders January 1. If you like, we can duplicate the initial six dresses so you'll have them to display for the Valentine's Day bridal event in February."

The Hearts Forever Bridal Fair. It's a huge shindig that lasts four days and Rosie and I are already planning our booth. Brides come from all over the South to attend and Thornhollow is hosting this year. Now, I can also display my designs and take orders.

I silently jump up and down, mentally squealing. "That's amazing," I tell her. "I'll get my website up and running as soon as possible, and I'll need professional pictures with models and such for each of the dresses."

I'm staring out the front window, all three cats making themselves comfortable in the displays. I see Logan leave his place across the street, Moxley in tow, and it's as if he knows I'm watching.

Our eyes meet and he blows me a kiss.

I raise my hand to catch it and press it to my heart. The diamond bracelet flashes rainbows on the walls and ceiling.

"I'll let you go, *cherie*, so you can enjoy the day," Gloria says. "Let's connect next week so you can see them and we'll make plans to get the photo shoot scheduled."

We disconnect after wishing each other a Merry Christmas, and I turn to glance over my shoulder at Persephone. "Thank you."

Without meeting my eye, she waves a hand through the air. "Go enjoy your family time. Tomorrow's another day."

Something in her voice tells me she didn't pop in to find out about Sherlock. There's more to this visit than she's letting on.

"What is it?" I ask.

"Hmm?"

"What aren't you telling me?"

"Nothing." She brushes at a throw pillow. "It can wait. Go. Have fun."

Great. She's baited me into spoiling the day, whether I demand she tell me what's going on or walk out the door not knowing.

I stomp to the fireplace. "Just tell me now."

Logan enters. "Are you ready?"

"Almost," I greet him. "Could you take that bag with the gifts to the car for me?"

He does and I return to grilling my guardian angel. "Tell. Me."

She sits forward, her overly make-upped eyes serious. "The event—that bridal fair? It'll be moved from the current planned location at the school gymnasium to the hotel two blocks over."

I don't ask how she knows—she's tapped into the divine hotline. "Okay, it will be at the Peach Time Inn. Big deal."

"The hotel is haunted."

Super. "Lots of places are around here."

"You don't want to go there, Ava. Too dangerous."

"Why is that?"

The front door opens and Logan's back. "Anything else?"

I heave a sigh but decide not to let Persephone and her doom and gloom further dampen my day. "We'll finish this discussion when I get back," I tell her, knowing she's about to do a disappearing act on me again.

Moxley peers at me from the Porsche passenger seat as Logan touches my cheek and gives me a kiss at my car. He's going to his own family celebration for their morning Christmas ritual. "I'm happy your mom and dad are back together," he says.

"Me, too." He opens the driver's door for me and I get in. "See you tonight."

He leans down and steals another kiss. "Can't wait."

I drive off with my heart full of excitement for the coming year.

The local radio station plays one of Dad's original holiday songs from a few years back. His new one is sure to be a hit as well. I sing along, so grateful he's alive, safe, and not in jail.

Even though the sun is shining, a few flakes begin to fall and swirl on the road.

Snow for Christmas. What else could I ask for?

I arrive at Mama's, hug both parents, and sit beside the

Christmas tree, confident our new life together is going to be perfect.

Except for the ghost of Rosie's grandmother who pops in and starts babbling about baby names. "*She should name it after me!*" Grandma exclaims.

Before I can tell her to go bug her granddaughter, a certain guardian angel appears.

"One other thing I forgot..." Persephone says, eyeing the assorted wrapped gifts. "That woman, Gloria?"

Mama and Daddy are in the kitchen getting hot chocolate for all of us, the sound of her laughter echoing into the room.

"Jeez. Really? Can't any of you leave me alone for a day? One day! That's all I'm asking for."

Grandma says something in Spanish that sounds a lot like a curse word. She vanishes.

The angel hits me with a look that rivals Mama's when I'm being impertinent.

"Fine. What about Gloria?"

"She's got a ghost problem of epic proportions, Ava. You're going to need a lot of help with that one."

Mama bustles in with a tray of three Santa mugs, matching tea pot, and a bag of marshmallows. The smell of warm chocolate mixes with the scent from the fir tree, and thank goodness, she and dad are oblivious to the angel.

Persephone eyes the cocoa as if she wishes she could partake. Then she begins to fade away. "Merry Christmas, spirit walker... See you soon..."

Books by Nyx

Sister Witches Of Raven Falls Mystery Series

Of Potions and Portents
Of Curses and Charms
Of Stars and Spells
Of Spirits and Superstition

Confessions of a Closet Medium Cozy Mystery Series
Pumpkins & Poltergeists
Magic & Mistletoe
Haunts & Hearts (February 2021)

Once Upon a Witch Cozy Mystery Series
If the Cursed Shoe Fits (Cinder)
Beastly Book of Spells (Belle) September 2020
Poisoned Apple Potion (Snow) October 2020
Red Hot Wolfie (Ruby) 2021
Hexed Hair Day (Rapunzel) 2021

About the Author

Nyx Halliwell is a writer from the South who grew up on TV shows like Buffy the Vampire Slayer and Charmed. She loves writing magical stories as much as she loves baking and crafting. She believes cats really can talk, but don't tell her three rescue puppies that.

She enjoys binge-watching mystery shows with her hubby and reading all types of stories involving magic and animals.

Connect with Nyx today and see pictures of her pets, be the first to know about new books and sales, and find out when Godfrey, the talking cat, has a new blog post! Receive a FREE copy of the Whitethorne Book of Spells and Recipes by signing up for her newsletter http://eepurl.com/gwKHB9

Connect with Nyx today!

FREE ebook with newsletter signup!!

Website: nyxhalliwell.com

Instagram: https://www.instagram.com/nyxhalliwellauthor/
Email: nyxhalliwellauthor@gmail.com
Bookbub https://www.bookbub.com/profile/nyx-halliwell
Amazon amazon.com/author/nyxhalliwell

Facebook: https://www.facebook.com/NyxHalliwellAuthor/
Twitter: @HalliwellNyx

Sign up for Nyx's Cozy Clues Mystery Newsletter and be the
FIRST to learn about new releases, sales, behind-the-scenes
trivia about the book characters, pictures of Nyx's pets, and
links to insightful and often hilarious *From the Cauldron With
Godfrey blog*! BONUS: a free ebook featuring recipes, crafts, and
fun magick!

Dear Reader

I hope you enjoyed this story!

As a real-life medium, this plot is based on a haunted necklace a couple brought me several years ago, with the spirit of a man trapped in it. Let me tell you, it was quite a session! I've never had anything like it since.

If you found the story entertaining, and would be so kind, would you leave a review on Goodreads and your favorite book retailer? I would REALLY appreciate it!

A review lets hundreds, if not thousands, of potential readers know what you enjoyed about the book, and helps them make wise buying choices. It's the best word-of-mouth around.

The review doesn't have to be anything long! Pretend you're telling a friend about the story. Pick out one or more characters, scenes, or dialogue that made you smile, laugh, or warmed your heart, and tell them about it. Just a few sentences is perfect!

Blessed be,

Nyx 🤍

Printed in the USA
CPSIA information can be obtained
at www.ICGtesting.com
LVHW021936040923
757128LV00036B/813